Letters from Skye

BALLANTINE BOOKS

NEW YORK

Letters from Skye

A NOVEL

Jessica Brockmole

Published in the United States by Ballantine Books,
an imprint of The Random House Publishing Group,
a division of Random House, Inc., New York.

BALLANTINE and colophon are registered
trademarks of Random House, Inc.

ISBN 978-0-345-54260-1
ebook ISBN 978-0-345-54261-8

Printed in the United States of America on acid-free paper

www.ballantinebooks.com

2 4 6 8 9 7 5 3 1

FIRST EDITION

Book design by Dana Leigh Blanchette
Title-page photograph: © iStockphoto

My breath,
      my light,
            the one my heart flies toward.

For Jim.

Letters from Skye

Chapter One

~

Elspeth

Urbana, Illinois, U.S.A.
March 5, 1912

Dear Madam,

I hope you won't think me forward, but I wanted to write to express my admiration for your book, *From an Eagle's Aerie*. I'll admit, I'm not usually a guy for poetry. More often, I can be found with a dog-eared copy of *Huck Finn* or something else involving mortal peril and escape. But something in your poems touched me more than anything has in years.

I've been in the hospital, and your little book cheered me better than the nurses. Especially the nurse with the mustache like my uncle Phil's. She's also touched me more than anything has in years, though in a much less exciting way. Generally I'm pestering the doctors to let me up and about so I can go back to my plotting. Just last week I painted the dean's horse blue, and I had hoped to bestow the same on his terrier. But with your book in hand, I'm content to stay as long as they keep bringing the orange Jell-O.

Most of your poems are about tramping down life's fears and climbing that next peak. As you can probably guess, there are few things that shake my nerves (apart from my hirsute nurse and her persistent thermometer). But writing a letter, uninvited, to a published author such as yourself—this feels by far my most daring act.

I am sending this letter to your publisher in London and will cross my fingers that it finds its way to you. And if I can ever repay you for your inspiring poetry—by painting a horse, for example—you only have to say the word.

> With much admiration,
> David Graham

Isle of Skye
25 March 1912

Dear Mr. Graham,

You should have seen the stir in our tiny post office, everyone gathered to watch me read my first letter from a "fan," as you Americans would say. I think the poor souls thought no one outside our island had ever laid eyes on my poetry. I don't know which was more thrilling to them—that someone had indeed read one of my books or that the someone was an American. You're all outlaws and cowboys, aren't you?

I myself admit to some surprise that my humble little works have fled as far as America. *From an Eagle's Aerie* is one of my more recent books, and I wouldn't have thought it had time to wing across the ocean yet. However you've acquired it, I'm just glad to know I'm not the only one who's read the blasted thing.

In gratitude,

Elspeth Dunn

Urbana, Illinois, U.S.A.

April 10, 1912

Dear Miss Dunn,

I don't know which made me giddier—to hear that *From an Eagle's Aerie* was among your "most recent books" or to get a response at all from such an esteemed poet. Surely you're too busy counting meter or compiling a list of scintillating synonyms (brilliant, sparkling, dazzling synonyms). Me, I spend my days robbing banks with the James Gang and the other outlaws and cowboys.

I was sent your book by a friend of mine who is up at Oxford. To my shock and dismay, I have not seen your works in print here in the United States. Even a thorough search of my university library turned up nothing. Now that I know you have others lurking on the bookstore shelves, I will have to appeal to my pal to send more.

I was astonished to read that mine was your first "fan" letter. I was sure it would be just one in a stack, which is why I went to such pains to make it fascinating and witty. Perhaps other readers haven't been as bold (or perhaps as impulsive?) as I.

Regards,

David Graham

P.S. Wherever is the Isle of Skye?

Isle of Skye
1 May 1912

Mr. Graham,

You don't know where my lovely isle is? Ridiculous! That would be like me saying I've never heard of Urbana, Illinois.

My isle is off the northwest coast of Scotland. A wild, pagan, green place of such beauty that I couldn't imagine being anywhere else. Enclosed is a picture of Peinchorran, where I live, with my cottage nestled between the hills around the loch. I'll have you know that, in order to draw this for you, I had to hike around the loch, trudge up the sheep path on the opposite hill, and find a patch of grass not covered by heather or sheep excreta. I'll expect you to do likewise when you send me a picture of Urbana, Illinois.

Do you lecture in Urbana? Study? I'm afraid I don't know what it is that Americans do at university.

Elspeth Dunn

P.S. By the way, it's "Mrs. Dunn."

Urbana, Illinois, U.S.A.
June 17, 1912

Dear *Mrs.* Dunn (please excuse my presumption!),

You draw as well as write such magnificent poetry? The picture you sent is sublime. Is there nothing you can't do?

As I can't draw worth a dime, I'm sending a few picture postcards instead. One is the auditorium at the university; the second is the tower on the library building. Not bad, huh? Illinois is probably as different from the Isle of Skye as a place could be. Not a mountain in sight. Once I leave campus, just corn as far as the eye can see.

I suppose I do what any collegiate American does: study, eat too much pie, torment the dean and his horse. I'm finishing up my studies in natural sciences. My father hopes I'll enter medical school and join him in his practice one day. I'm not as certain about my future as he seems to be. For now, I'm just trying to make it through my last year of college with my sanity intact!

David Graham

Isle of Skye
11 July 1912

Mr. Graham,

"Is there nothing you can't do?" you ask. Well, I can't dance. Or tan leather. Or make barrels or shoot a harpoon. And I'm not particularly good at cooking. Can you believe I burned *soup* the other day? But I can sing fairly well, shoot a straight shot

from a rifle, play the cornet (can't we all?), and I'm something
of an amateur geologist. And, although I couldn't cook a decent
roast lamb if my life depended on it, I make a marvellous
Christmas pudding.

Forgive my frankness, but why devote all of your time (and
sanity) towards an area of study that doesn't grip your very
soul? If I had had a chance to go to university, I wouldn't have
spent even a moment on a subject that didn't interest me.

I should love to think I would've spent my university days
reading poetry, as there's no better way to pass the time, but
after so many years masquerading as a "real poet," there likely
isn't much a professor could teach me now.

No, as unladylike as it sounds, I would have studied geology.
My older brother Finlay is always out on the water and brings
me rocks smooth from the ocean. I can't help but wonder where
they came from and how they washed up on the Western Isles.

There, now you know my secret wishes! I shall have to take
your firstborn child in exchange. Or I suppose I could settle for
a secret of your own. If you weren't studying natural science,
what would you be studying? What do you wish you could be
doing with your life above all?

Elspeth

Urbana, Illinois, U.S.A.
August 12, 1912

Dear Rumpelstiltskin,

If you teach me to play the cornet, I'll teach you to dance!

I don't think there is anything unladylike about geology.
Why is it that you never escaped your isle for college? If I had
lived in a more geologically interesting place than central Illinois, I might have considered a similar field. I'd always hoped to
study American literature—Twain, Irving, and the like—but
my father refused to pay for me to spend four years "reading
stories."

But what I wish to do above all? That's an easy question, but
the answer is not one I'm willing to admit. I'm afraid you'll have
to accept my firstborn child after all.

David

Isle of Skye
1 September 1912

Mr. Graham,

Well, now my interest is piqued! What is it that you always
longed to be as a wee boy? A naval captain? A circus acrobat? A
traveling perfume salesman? You must, must tell, or I shall form
speculations of my own. I am a poet, after all, and I live amidst
people who believe in fairies and ghosts. My imagination is
quite fertile.

You asked why I didn't go to university somewhere off the isle, and I have a confession to make. Now, this is quite embarrassing, mind you.

Let me take a deep breath.

I've never been off Skye. My whole life. Really! The reason is . . . well, I'm afraid of boats. I can't swim and am afraid to get into the water to even learn. I know you are probably falling from your desk chair, laughing. A person who lives on an island, utterly terrified of the water? But there you have it. Not even the lure of university could convince me to step foot on a boat. Oh, I tried. Really I did! I had actually planned to sit for a scholarship exam. I even had my suitcase all packed. Finlay and I, we were going to give it a go together. But when I eyed that ferry . . . oh, it just didn't look seaworthy. It doesn't seem *right* that boats float on the water. No amount of whisky could entice me on.

There! Now you have *two* secrets of mine. You know about my ridiculous aspirations towards geology and my even more ridiculous fear of the water and of boats. Now you surely can feel safe confiding your secret to me. You really can trust me, if for no other reason than there is no one else (apart from the sheep) for me to tell.

    Elspeth

P.S. Please stop calling me "Mrs. Dunn."

Chapter Two

~

Margaret

The Borders
Tuesday, 4 June 1940

Dearest Mother,

That's another batch delivered! I swear, there must not be
a single child left in all of Edinburgh with all we've evacuated
to the countryside away from those bombs. These three were
better than most; at least they could reliably wipe their own
noses.

I have to get this group settled and then I promised Mrs.
Sunderland I'd pay a wee visit to her brood in Peebles. Any letters from Paul?

Love and kisses,
Margaret

Edinburgh
8 June 1940

Margaret,

You're running yourself ragged; you've only just come back from Aberdeenshire! Most lasses stay in one place, rolling bandages or building battleships or whatever it is that young women do these days. But there you are, tramping up and down the Scottish countryside like the Pied Piper, with all of those poor children running after. Don't they know you can't tell one end of the compass from the other? And that it was only recently *you* could reliably wipe your own nose?

But, no, dearest, no letters from Paul. Have faith. If there's one thing you can expect from that boy, it's a letter. And then about a hundred more.

> Stay safe,
> Your Mother

Still the Borders
Wednesday, 12 June 1940

Dear Mother,

If my best friend can go flying about Europe with the R.A.F., then whyever can't I fly about Scotland?

But you haven't heard from him, have you? Everyone keeps saying the R.A.F. wasn't at Dunkirk, but Paul said, "I'll be right back," and then hasn't written since. Where else would he have gone? So either he's out of stamps or he hasn't come back from France.

But, really, I'm trying not to worry. The little ones, they fret enough away from their mothers; I don't want to upset them more.

I'm for Peebles in the morning and then on to Edinburgh from there. Have tea and cakes from Mackie's bakery waiting for me! Else I may just stay on the train until I get to Inverness . . .

Love and kisses,
Margaret

Edinburgh
15 June 1940

Margaret,

If I knew all it would take to lure you home was a dish of Mackie's cakes, I would've tried it ages ago, sugar ration or no!

Still nothing from Paul. But you can't depend on the mail in wartime. I don't remember you worrying so much about him before. Isn't he just a pen friend?

Mother

Peebles
Monday, 17 June 1940

Mother,

Yes, I'm still here in Peebles. The trains are a muddle and
I've had a very persistent Annie Sunderland trying to convince
me to pop her in my suitcase and bring her along to Edinburgh.
When I threaten to paste her feet to the floor, she begs for just
one story more. You know her, with those big brown eyes. How
can I resist? Of course she misses her mummy, but the family
Annie and the boys stay with here are just wonderful. I can
bring back a good report to Mrs. Sunderland.

I suppose I should tell you, Paul may be a bit more than a
pen friend. At least that's how he sees it. He fancies he's in love
with me. I think he's quite ridiculous and I've told him so.
We're merely friends. Best friends, to be sure. You remember
how we'd always go hiking and bouldering and then share a
sandwich. But in love? I didn't tell you before because I was
sure you'd laugh. He *is* being ridiculous, isn't he?

I should be home tomorrow or the next, if I have to walk
every step of the way from Peebles. Onward!

Love and kisses,

Margaret

POST OFFICE TELEGRAM
18.06.40 PLYMOUTH

MARGARET DUNN, EDINBURGH
MAISIE NO WORRIES I AM SAFE=
SHORT LEAVE IN PLYMOUTH=
THINKING OF YOU=
    PAUL+

Mother!

He's written!

I saw the telegram propped up on the table and I couldn't wait for you to come home from church. I worried I might miss the train south. I wrapped up all of the cakes. They will be quite a treat for him. I hope you don't mind.

My suitcase and I are heading right back to Waverley Station. I'll write to you when I get there.

He's written.

    Margaret

Edinburgh
18 June 1940

Oh, my Margaret,

I know I can never send this letter; it'll end up on the grate the moment I put words to paper. If you only knew how my heart wrenches to read your note on the table, amidst the crumbs on the empty cake plate. If you knew how it feels to run after someone for a brief snatch of time, how the world stops spinning, just for a moment, when you hold them in your arms, and then starts again so fast that you fall to the ground, dizzy. If you knew how every hello hurts more than a hundred goodbyes. If you knew.

But you don't. I never told you. You have no secrets from me, but I've kept a part of myself locked away, always. A part of me that started scratching at the wall the day this other war started, that started howling to get out right now, the day you ran off to meet your soldier.

I should have told you, should've taught you to steel your heart. Taught you that a letter isn't always just a letter. Words on the page can drench the soul. If only you knew.

Mother

Chapter Three

~

Elspeth

Urbana, Illinois, U.S.A.
September 21, 1912

Dear Elspeth,

If not "Mrs. Dunn," what, then? What is it that your friends call you? Ellie? Libby? Elsie? Around here I'm known as "Mort" (don't ask), but my mother calls me "Davey."

You've never been off Skye? I don't know why I should find that so unbelievable. I mean, there will always be people with a fear of the sea, and someone who lives so close to the sea would see firsthand how frightening it can be. Have you never even crossed over a bridge?

Okay, do you really want to know my secret? My parents don't know this, and my friends would bust a gut if they heard. Here goes: If I could be anything in the world, I would be a dancer. A ballet dancer, like Nijinsky. I saw him dance in Paris

and it was amazing! Actually, "amazing" doesn't do it justice. I
went every night that I could get a seat, no matter how far from
the stage I was. I didn't know it was possible for a human to
jump and twirl as high as he did. And he made it all look so ef-
fortless! I've never had any lessons, but I've always been
thought of as a fair dancer. Perhaps the next Nijinsky?

There! Now you have it! You hold my social future in the
palms of your hands.

I think I can hear the laughter all the way from Scotland. . . .

Must go—the tree wars are beginning!

Regards,

David

Isle of Skye
10 October 1912

Davey,

Marvellous! This world needs more male ballet dancers, just
as it needs more female geologists.

And what, pray tell, is a tree war? Is Urbana, Illinois, so ar-
boreally poor that its citizens must go to war? Trees are scarce
on Skye, to be sure, but we don't actually have to do battle. If
the situation is that dire, please let me know. I will post a sapling
or two.

The seas here are said to be inhabited by the *each uisge,* a
water horse who pulls his victims beneath the sea and tears them
apart with his fangs until only the liver is left, floating up omi-

nously to the surface. Raised on stories like this, what could entice me to step foot in the water?

Really, though, I do have my reasons. The sea can be terrifying. My da is a fisherman. My brother Alasdair was too but one day never came home. His boat did, scattered on the shingle in bits and pieces. So, yes, I do understand the dangers of the sea.

If there was a bridge connecting Skye to the mainland, perhaps I might have left. But, until that day comes, as long as I have the ferry to contend with, I fear I shall always be a prisoner on my island.

Elspeth

P.S. As strange as it may sound, my friends call me "Elspeth." But you, not knowing me well enough yet to be a friend, may call me whatever you like.

Urbana, Illinois, U.S.A.
November 3, 1912

Whatever I like? Then Sue it is!

Tree wars? They're silly pranks. Every class plants a tree on the campus and then the other classes try to destroy it. My class has already lost one. We've planted anew and have high hopes for the newest member of the '13s. We're guarding it in shifts, armed with eggs and paper sacks filled with water. Danny Norton has been feeding the tree a formula he swears by, but I think it's mostly beer with a bit of bay rum oil to mask the scent. It must be working, as the tree hasn't kicked it yet. The other night we yanked up the '14s' sapling, roots and all!

Despite the tree wars, things aren't all fun and games around here. This term is already turning out to be pretty difficult. My friends think the senior year is the easiest of all, but I have such a heavy load of courses. I'm at the library so often, I'm considering moving my pillow and toothbrush over. What's easy about it? I'm dreading exam time.

You know, it's times like this that I doubt the future. I kept hoping that at some point the right professor or course would inflame me and I'd feel the passion others seem to feel. That I'd know, without question, what I wanted to spend the rest of my life doing. But here I am, my final year of college, and I still really have no idea.

I always assumed I'd follow my father into medicine. Well, I suppose *he's* always assumed that and I've just followed suit, having no plan of my own. I've come to realize, though, that I'm not eager for it. As much as I hate school, I almost wish I could just stay. Then I wouldn't have to go out into the "big, wide world."

Well, there, you've heard my worries and my doubts. Perhaps they're born of frustration as I move closer to end-of-term exams. I'm sorry to burden you with such glum ponderings. I'll have to send this letter quickly before I change my mind.

Tired,
David

Isle of Skye
23 November 1912

Davey,

Don't go jumping off your library tower, please!

We're not always made for doing the same as the others. My brother Finlay, he could carve the *Mona Lisa* on an acorn if he wanted to. I'd just end up with a splinter. I could never be a Nijinsky, no matter how hard I was to try. Those classmates with passion and aptitude for their field of study, it's what they were made to do. Davey, you can't force yourself to be the same. You're made for something on this earth, but maybe it's not what your father thinks. Does he know how unhappy you are?

In my book, your aptitude lies in keeping a Scottish recluse from going mad during an island winter. The sheep aren't nearly as fascinating.

Really, though, Davey, you have passion. There's something out there for you. Hold fast to that hope. You'll find it.

Elspeth

Urbana, Illinois, U.S.A.
December 11, 1912

Sue,

Your letter offered me a much-welcome break from studying. It even helped to soothe my throbbing head. I was in the hospital recently and still am not quite up to snuff.

I'm not sure if my parents know how I feel about school.

When I was starting college and mentioned I'd fancy studying American literature, my father actually laughed. Didn't even look up from his newspaper. Just laughed and said, "Ridiculous." He has a big walrus mustache, and when he laughs, he doesn't make a sound. You only know because the tips of his mustache twitch. There he sat, sniffing, mustache twitching, saying things like "Ridiculous" and "No career in that." "But I enjoy literature," I protested. "Medicine. That's what you need to study. You'll thank me for it later. Nothing more rewarding."

I really did try to tell him then, Sue, honest I did. But it only bloomed into an argument, with my mother wringing her hands and imploring me to just "give it a try." My father finally thumped his newspaper down and declared that he wasn't paying for that nonsense and that, if I wanted to study something frivolous like literature, it wouldn't be on his dime.

So you see why I can't talk to my parents. I need to just carry on. Finish college, finish medical school. Once I get a job, I can make my own decisions. Maybe.

I should get back to my studying. I'm looking forward to the holidays as a time to rest up and recuperate before the term starts up again.

> Eyes swimming, vision blurring,
> David

Isle of Skye
5 January 1913

Dear David,

Happy New Year! It has been so cold, I can barely tear myself from my spot in front of the fire. When I finally did bundle
myself and trudge to the post office, I found a letter from you
waiting, and so it was well worth the trip.

How was your holiday? We try to make it merry around
here. I made my famous Christmas pudding and had the bonniest wee Christmas tree, strung with ropes of dried flowers.
Boughs of evergreen lay across the mantelpiece and swung
above the doorways. I was given a pair of mittens, a new kettle,
and one of Robert W. Service's books. Have you read his
poetry? Simply marvellous stuff. If you enjoy reading my little
verses, you should dip into his.

What are some of your favourite books? Like any whose
blood runs tartan, I adore W. S. Indeed, I don't know that I
could call myself an islander if I hadn't read *The Lord of the Isles*.
I think his novels are sometimes a bit too Gothic for my tastes,
but his poetry really does a fine job of capturing Scotland in all
of her changeable moods. I have a cheerful fondness for my battered copy of *Alice's Adventures in Wonderland,* the first book I
ever owned. My brothers and I would run Caucus-races down
on the shingle while shouting the driest things we knew into the
wind. And I'm almost embarrassed to admit that I've just read
and quite enjoyed *Three Weeks*. You probably wouldn't have
guessed me for an Elinor Glyn sort of girl.

Elspeth

P.S. I'm so sorry to hear that you've been in hospital. I hope it's nothing serious. You seem to do this with alarming frequency.

Urbana, Illinois, U.S.A.
February 1, 1913

Dear Sue,

My holidays were splendid! I was in Chicago with my parents. My sister, Evie, and her husband came up from Terre Haute and I met my new little niece, Florence, for the first time. She's almost a year old now. Full of smiles and the most infectious giggles as she yanked on my suspenders. I bought her a doll in a silk dress, which she was obviously too young for, as all she did was chew on the doll's hand and laugh at me. I'll probably still be buying her dolls in silk dresses when she's far too old for them, and she'll likely still be laughing at me.

I got a box camera for Christmas. Here's a picture of me, so you can see your humble correspondent. Now you'll have to respond likewise! Also, more handkerchiefs than I can ever hope to need, courtesy of my mother, a crisp copy of *Gray's Anatomy* from my dad, and a set of stereo cards of the British Isles. This last was a special request; I want to see more of the land you call home. And finally, from my sister, one of your earlier books, which she amazingly tracked down somewhere. She stole a peek before wrapping it up, and I'm afraid you have another convert! Now that the new term has begun, I've been rationing myself with a poem a night, with the whole saved as a sort of reward for a job well done on my midterm exams.

My favorite books? Without a doubt, Mark Twain is my favorite author, but to pick just one of his books? I don't know if it can be done! Of course, none can compare to *Huckleberry Finn*, but *A Connecticut Yankee* is rollicking. I suppose about as far from your Lewis Carroll as one can get, though I confess I've read *Through the Looking-Glass* forward and back. I do like Jack London, Wilkie Collins, and H. Rider Haggard. Stories full of mystery and adventure. Poe can't be beat for a thrill. I like a good western too and read things like Zane Grey when I want to take a break from "literature." And who is "W. S." if not Will Shakespeare? I'm afraid I've never read *The Lord of the Isles*.

No, I wouldn't have pegged you for an Elinor Glyn sort of girl. I have only a passing acquaintance with her books. And I do literally mean "passing," as *Three Weeks* circulated from room to room in my dorm. One enterprising young man found a faux tiger skin rug for his floor, hoping, perhaps, "to sin/With Elinor Glyn." She never paid a visit to our dorm, nor do I remember any other ladies taking him up on the offer.

How did I end up in the hospital? Well . . . I was trying to ride a cow and fell off. Cow-riding isn't a risky sport in itself—I've done it on numerous occasions—but we were leading the cow up the stairs of the Natural History Building toward the president's office. She wasn't as keen on the idea. I can only say that I don't recommend this as a form of transportation. And what do you mean, I end up in the hospital a lot?

Back to the grindstone, with a new term. I can't say that this term is looking to be any easier than the last, but at least I'm almost finished!

Refreshed,

David

Isle of Skye

27 February 1913

Dear David,

Many thanks for the picture. You look so serious! And much younger than I thought. I can see a glint in your eye, though, that suggests a boy capable of stealing a tree or riding a cow. What became of your class tree?

Don't look for a picture from me. No camera over here, and I don't think I could draw myself objectively. I would keep modifying and erasing until you had a picture of Princess Maud. We always want to appear more attractive than we really are, don't you think? I mean, if you had been sketching your picture instead of snapping it with a camera, would you really have drawn in that dreadful checked jacket?

Now that I've seen your picture, I can imagine you and your mates passing around *Three Weeks*. You wait on tenterhooks for your turn, and when you get the book in your eager hands, you race to your room, homework forgotten for the night. And as you start reading, your cheeks get quite pink as you realise just how unlike Henry James this is.

I've never read Mark Twain, but I agree that Poe is thrilling.

I remember reading "The Tell-Tale Heart" as a girl one night, in bed with a candle stub I pilfered from church. I was certainly punished for stealing the candle, because after I finished the book and blew out the candle, I couldn't sleep a wink. I was quite positive that I heard the beating of the heart downstairs. When dawn broke, my mother found me sitting stiffly in bed, quite awake, clutching my blanket around me. I was convinced God was punishing me for my sin of stealing the altar candle. So what did I do the following Sunday to atone for my sin? I pilfered a candle from our cupboard at home and left it at the church!

And, dear boy, W. S. is, of course, Walter Scott. I'm sure they have a few of his knocking around that enormous university library of yours. Regardless, if you've read *Through the Looking-Glass* more than once, you and I will get on beautifully. "Jabberwocky" is my favourite.

In your very first letter (yes, I save all your letters!), you spoke of having been in hospital recently. What sort of livestock had you been using inappropriately at that time? Trying to waltz with a horse? Play football with a ram?

Elspeth

Urbana, Illinois, U.S.A.
March 21, 1913

Dear Sue,

I had to put aside my books to answer immediately and defend myself and my poor checked jacket. You obviously have no sense of style on the Isle of Skye, as my jacket and I are at the height of fashion here on campus! And I had to look serious in the picture; it's my first mustache. I'm curious now, how old do you think I look?

All right, if you won't sit in front of the mirror and draw me a picture with your pencil, please sit in front of the mirror and draw me a picture with your words. Look in the mirror, right now, and tell me what it is that you see. I'll put together my own picture.

No, no previous abuses of livestock, at least not any that landed me in the hospital. That earlier hospital visit was due to trying to scale the walls of the Women's Building and sneak into Alice McGinty's room. I shinnied up the drainpipe and had almost made it to the top when my hands slipped. My leg was broken and so was my heart, as Alice didn't even appreciate my effort. I can understand her displeasure, as she was nearly kicked out of the dormitory over the incident. And do you know the most frustrating part of it all? I had climbed that very same drainpipe on more than one occasion, often with a jar of grasshoppers tied in my jacket or, on one memorable evening, a sack of squirrels.

And our tree (we christened him "Paulie") is still inching up. We may win this war yet!

I was quite shocked when you said you had never read Mark Twain. What sort of education do you get in Scotland? This is a deficiency I shall have to rectify. Please accept this copy of *Huck Finn*—as a belated Christmas gift, if you like—excusing its battered appearance. I found it in a secondhand bookshop and it

appears quite well loved, if recently kicked to the curb.
I couldn't give it a good home, already having a copy above
my desk, but knew I could entrust you with its well-being.

    Until next time,
    David

Isle of Skye
9 April 1913

Dear David,

    And what a splendid mustache it is!

    Oh, I am so *horrid* at guessing ages. I think with those round
cheeks (so perfect for pinching, Davey-boy!) and that lock of
hair falling into your face, you look about eighteen or so. A lady
never reveals her age, but I'm not much older.

    All right, sir, I will attempt your challenge. And I will try to
be honest with my description as well.

    Looking in the mirror, what do I see? I have a thin face and
somewhat pointed chin. Small nose, narrow lips. My hair is
brown and as straight as a line. I have it pulled back in a knot
low on my head, as severe as I can make it, but it is so fine that I
already have strands escaping and flying about my face. My eyes
are the amber colour of my da's good malt whisky. Although
Màthair (that's Gaelic for "Mother") tries to keep me neat, I
tend to wear my brothers' old sweaters and skirts far too short
to be fashionable. Don't tell, but I've even been known to wear
a pair of trousers—tailored down to my size—when out hiking.

There! What do you think? Can you picture me? If I had sketched that for you, I certainly would've padded out the bosom.

A sack full of squirrels, Davey? My, but you are a scamp! Those poor women. Why do these things if they end in yet another visit to the fine medical facilities of Urbana, Illinois?

I was quite excited to get the copy of *Huckleberry Finn*. I don't have much of a library and so any book, no matter how battered, is welcome. Books get read and reread during those long Scottish winter nights.

Elspeth

Chapter Four

~

Margaret

Plymouth
Wednesday, 19 June 1940

Dear Mother,

You can give it to me. I ran out without even saying good-bye. And after a boy who, until recently, was nothing more than a pen friend. And a poor pen friend at that, what with the weeks of not hearing from him. But if you could have seen how sweet and plaintive he looked waiting at the station, you would've forgiven him too!

He's well but had a near miss. Nothing worse than a few scrapes and a sprained wrist, though he won't tell me what happened. Just that he's glad to see me and feels better already.

I don't have any vackies scheduled to escort, so, if you don't

mind, I'll stay down here for a bit. Paul doesn't know when
he'll next get leave and, Mother, he needs me.

    Love and kisses,
    Margaret

Edinburgh
22 June 1940

My Margaret,

    You don't know how I worried about you, traveling all the way
to Plymouth by yourself. You've never been so far from home.

    Perhaps you shouldn't stay longer. You've gone down,
you've cheered up your friend and satisfied yourself that he is as
well as can be. You've even brought him every last crumb of the
precious cakes bought with my ration coupons. You should
come home now. You should come home before this becomes
anything serious. Please.

    Love,
    Mother

Plymouth
Thursday, 27 June 1940

Mother,

    I know you love me, but I'm old enough to decide on my
own. And, besides, things have already become serious. Paul
asked me to marry him.

    Margaret

Edinburgh
1 July 1940

Margaret,

Don't make any rash decisions. Not for my sake; for
yours. It's been half a year since you've been in the same
city as Paul. There were days when the two of you couldn't
stop bickering. And then all this love and marriage out of
nowhere?

It's the war talking. I know; I've seen it. They head off,
invincible, feeling as if the future is a golden pool before
them, ready to dive into. And then something happens—a
bomb, a sprained wrist, a bullet that whizzes by too close for
comfort—and suddenly they are grabbing for whatever they
can hold on to. That golden pool, it swirls around them, and
they worry they might drown if they're not careful. They hold
tight and make whatever promise comes to mind. You can't believe anything said in wartime. Emotions are as fleeting as a
quiet night.

Please be careful. Last week, we had planes overhead. One
dropped five bombs and more than a hundred incendiaries
around Craigmillar Castle. Nothing on the city, thank God, but
the planes go right above us. Two nights, crouched down in
the neighbourhood shelter in my dressing gown, hearing the
air-raid sirens and the growling engines and the rattle of
the anti-aircraft guns, but not really knowing what was happening. It's wearing on me. All I want is my Margaret by my
side.

Please don't make any decisions you'll regret later. Please

don't give away your heart without realizing it, because, my sweet girl, you may never get it back.

 Love,

 Mother

Plymouth

Friday, 5 July 1940

Mother,

 You always told me to reach out and grab happiness with both hands. Other mums pushed their daughters towards university or factory work or pouring tea in a NAAFI canteen. You didn't. You knew I'd be miserable. Instead, you found for me children needing an escort out to the country. I could escape the city just when it started to become crowded with pillboxes and Anderson shelters and home-guard exercises in the park. Those tromps in the Borders or the Highlands are pure happiness.

 I never said that I accepted Paul's offer. I told him I had to think on it. See? I'm not as rash as all that. But I'm *happy*, Mother. Just the way you always wish for me to be. I'll be home soon.

 Love and kisses,

 Margaret

Edinburgh
9 July 1940

Dear Margaret,

Thinking is good. It's what separates humans from cock-roaches.

Mother

Plymouth
Saturday, 13 July 1940

Dear Mother,

You'll be happy to know, Paul is all patched and rested and back to serve Fair Britannia on the morrow. I'll be starting to work my way north then, though I can't promise to the efficiency of the rails these days.

Love and kisses,
Margaret

Edinburgh
Thursday, 18 July 1940

Paul,

Mother is furious at us. Well, at me, really. It's preposterous! It's not as if we did anything shocking. It's just a ring, after all. A ring and a promise.

We've had a terrible row over it, though, so I'm up here on

the roof with this letter and no idea how to apologise. She said I was ridiculous for saying "yes" to the first boy who asked me. But then she said that, in war, happiness was hard to find. I told her *she* was the ridiculous one and she should make up her mind. What if the first boy to ask me *was* the one who made me happiest? Then she threw a spoon at me and said she just doesn't have all the answers.

So I crawled onto the roof to stew. She finally leaned out of her bedroom window and said that the war unsettled her. She'd already been through one, but this war came with the constant edge of fear, the nights when the air-raid sirens sounded, and the nights when they didn't. "War is impulsive," she said. "Don't spend the rest of your life looking for ghosts."

I asked what on earth she meant, but she turned away and wouldn't say a word. "You're talking about my da, aren't you?"

"I've told you before, there's nothing you need to know about him."

"And why not? He's my da."

You know it all, Paul. You've heard me rant and rant how she's never said a word about my father. How she always deflects my questions and says the past is past. And I understand what she means. I do. She raised me alone; she wants me to be satisfied with that. To treasure the time we have together. But to not know where I came from or how I came to be . . . you know all the questions I have.

While she hovered in the bedroom window, I said all of this. She tried to pass it by with a joke. "The first volume of my life is out of print," she's fond of saying.

But this time I didn't let her. I pushed back. Regrets? Ghosts?

She's never talked like that before. "Why won't you talk about him?" I asked. "What about him is so horrible that it makes you write him from your memory?"

I thought she'd pace and wring her hands, but she stood very still. "I have *never* forgotten him," she finally said. "But I'll remember for the both of us." Her eyes shone as she left.

I can hear her rummaging around in the kitchen now. Attempting to cook is (unfortunately) her form of apology. Whatever she's doing, it smells dreadful. I don't even want to think about which vegetable she's ruining right now.

I really should go in and tell her I'm sorry for calling her ridiculous. For even starting an argument at all. I should apologise for pushing her to tell me about my father, about the regrets, about the ghosts. I know she means well and is tired and just misses having me around. She's doing her best. I do treasure our time together.

Maybe I can convince her to go for a walk. Still a couple of hours until sunset. We can walk down to Holyrood Park, climb amongst the gorse. Blether about nothing in particular. Or maybe she'll be willing to talk now. I truly wonder . . .

Oh, goodness, Paul, I don't even know what I meant to write there. I can hardly believe what's happened. I heard the planes and just had time to tuck my notebook into my blouse before a bomb hit. Mother had written to me about all the recent air raids and the planes overhead, but I couldn't imagine it. I know life is different for you; you've had far too many nights broken by planes and sirens. But for me . . . A bomb? On the street where I used to skip as a child?

I saw it fall. . . . It spun straight onto the pavement, right out on the street. I ducked behind the dormer just in time. Rock and dirt kicked up everywhere. The cobbles were there one moment and the next were a smoking crater. I have no idea how I kept my balance, how I didn't fall off the roof with the blast. There wasn't even a siren.

I remembered Mother. The bedroom window had shattered, everything silent inside. I called her. I didn't know how to get into the room, with all the jagged glass around the window. Inside, all was shambles. The bed had skidded right up against the far wall, the night table on its side. A paving stone, flung through the window with perfect trajectory, had torn through a section of wainscoting. Papers fluttered white in the sunset-drenched room.

I called again and then I saw her shadow in the doorway. She stepped in slowly, her blue satin slippers toeing away the papers. But she didn't come all the way to the window. She just stood, staring at the splintered wainscoting and the snowfall of paper.

I reached through and yanked down one of the blackout curtains. I wrapped my hand and knocked out the glass around the windowsill so I could climb in.

Mother still didn't say a word. She dropped to the floor and pulled armfuls of paper onto her lap. I bent and picked one up. A letter, yellowed and creased, addressed to someone named Sue. And, because it sounds so much like you, Paul, I copy it here.

Chicago, Illinois, U.S.A.
October 31, 1915

Dear Sue,

I know you're angry; please don't be. Talk of "duty"
and "patriotism" aside, how could you really expect me to
pass up on this, the ultimate adventure?

My mother's been floating around the house, red-eyed
and sniffling. My father still isn't speaking to me. And yet
I feel as if I'm doing something right. I messed up in college. I messed up at work. Hell, I even messed up with
Lara. I was beginning to think there was no place in the
world for a guy whose highest achievement included a
sack full of squirrels. Nobody seemed to want my bravado and impulsivity before. You know this is right for
me, Sue. You of all people, who seem to know things
about me before I myself do. You know this is right.

I'm leaving tomorrow for New York and have to trust
my mother to mail this letter. When you read it, I'll be on
a ship somewhere in the Atlantic. Even though we get a
reduction on our fares if we sail the French Line, Harry
and I are bound for England. He has Minna over there
waiting for him. And I . . . I have you. Like knights of
old, neither of us can head off to fight without a token
from our love to tuck into our sleeve.

I'll be landing in Southampton sometime in the middle
of November and will be going up to London. Sue, say
that you'll meet me this time. I know it's easy for me to
ask, far easier than it is for you to leave your sanctuary up

on Skye. Don't let me go off to the front without having touched you for the first time, without having heard your voice say my name. Don't let me go off to the front without a memory of you in my heart.

    Yours . . . always and forever,
    Davey

"These are mine." Mother grabbed at other letters fluttering around. "You have no right to read them."

I asked what they were, who Sue was, but she didn't answer. She sat there with wet eyes, fumbling hands piling up the yellowing paper. Outside the windows, the air-raid sirens finally started.

"Go," she said finally, holding the envelopes tight. "Just go."

With the sounds of the sirens and the ack-ack guns, I stumbled from the house towards the air-raid shelter. I knew I had to finish the letter to you, that there was no one else I could tell about this evening. About how none of it seemed real.

I've never kept secrets from my mother. You know that, Paul. But as I hunkered down in that shelter, with my notebook still tucked in my blouse and the letter in my hand, I wondered what she'd kept from me.

    Margaret

Chapter Five

~

Elspeth

Chicago, Illinois, U.S.A.
June 17, 1913

Dear Sue,

I am finished!

I'm sorry it took me so long to respond, but I was waiting to be able to tell you that I'm completely and utterly done. Ah, what a luxury to sit down to write to you without a stack of books glaring at me from my desk! Instead, I'm sitting in my parents' house, window open, warm summer breeze puffing out the lace curtains, with nothing more malevolent glaring at me than the *Chicago Tribune*. Just to lean back, sip some cool lemonade, and write to you—extravagance itself!

You'll be quite proud of me, I think. I came clean with my father. You may wonder how I worked up the courage to tell him. By barely scraping by in my classes! He took one look at my grades and sniffed. "How do you expect to get into medical school with grades like this?" he asked. "I don't expect to," I said. "I don't expect to nor do I care." He nearly choked on his morning coffee. "What do you mean, you don't care?" "Exactly that, Father. I've never wanted to go to medical school. And it's too late now to convince me otherwise." He left the table with a thud of his chair and hasn't spoken to me since. I think it's only through my mother's good graces that he hasn't thrown me out on my ear.

My sister is here staying at my parents' for a time this summer, making it easier to handle my father's sulks, and I'm able to spend more time getting to know my niece, Florence. There's a spot in the sitting room in the back of the house where the sunlight falls through the window just so in the afternoon. Florence and I will sit in that circle of sunlight and watch each other. When she gets tired of staring at me with those great blue eyes of hers, she'll crawl onto my lap, tug on my suspenders, and beg, "Unc' Day! P'ease, story?" And how can I resist such a plea? I tell her a fairy story and watch her eyes grow large at the frightening parts and turn up in the corners when she is laughing. It is marvelous to see the raw play of emotions on the face of a child. No trying to conceal any feeling or disguise one emotion as something else. We are going to be great friends, my niece and I, I can already tell.

Another bit of news: I have a girl I've started stepping out with. Lara. She's a real nice girl, in college studying German literature. We met at a party, one of those socially tedious events one is expected to attend on occasion. I went to please my mother. Lara and I met and, after talking, realized that she

"knew" my parents. One of those convoluted acquaintances—
you know, where her mother plays bridge with my mother's best
friend's aunt Vivian, or some such nonsense. Whatever the acquaintance, it means my mother approves of her.

So, see, life is going wonderfully for me right now. Two girls
in my life, a room all to myself, and NO MORE EXAMS!

Oh, the night I dropped the squirrels in the Women's Building was a classic! Can you think of a much better combination
than a perilous climb, a gang of displaced squirrels, and shriek-
ing women in various states of undress? I must say, though,
these escapades don't often end in hospital visits. But it's
the possibility they *could* that makes the pranks so tempting
to me.

That's really where my nickname came from. The guys, they
call me "Mort," morbidly convinced that my antics will lead me
straight to the mortuary one day. Splendid fellows, aren't they?

How are things on Skye for you, Sue? You must be happier
with the snow gone. I can already picture you cheerfully tromp-
ing all over the hills in your trousers and hat, notebook tucked
under one arm, pencil stuck behind an ear. Ah, summer!

By the way, you didn't guess my age correctly. I'm already
twenty-one! Now you can see why I strove to grow that mustache. . . .

    Relaxed, relaxing,
    David

P.S. Here is a photo of me in all my robes and mortarboard.
That proud sapling next to me is Paulie. Both the tree and I have
(amazingly!) made it through the year!

Isle of Skye
7 July 1913

Dear David,

You look so exuberant! I don't know who looks prouder or
straighter—you or the tree. I'm glad things are going so well for
you.

Your niece sounds delightful, and you are lucky to be able to
see her as often as you do. My brother Alasdair died several
years ago, and his widow moved to Edinburgh with their children. I haven't seen Chrissie or my niece or nephews since then.
My two other brothers, Finlay and Willie, are still living at
home, so no children forthcoming there (at least, Màthair hopes
not!), although Finlay has a girl I think he's quite serious about,
so it may not be long. Kate's a sweet thing; we are all crossing
our fingers.

Now that you aren't going on to medical school, what are
you doing to fill your time? Have you joined up with the Ballets
Russes yet? Learned to play the cornet? Started writing the
Great American Novel?

I'm sure it's much easier to have a sweetheart now that your
evenings aren't full of studying. You say that Lara attends university. Is that usual for American women? All of the girls I went
to school with thought of nothing more than getting married,
picking out curtains, and basically emptying their heads of ten or
twelve years' worth of lessons. They thought I was as mad as a
March hare for even wanting to read a book not on the suggested
school curriculum, let alone wanting to attend university.

Elspeth

Chicago, Illinois, U.S.A.
July 27, 1913

Dear Sue,

No, I haven't joined the Ballet Russes. To be honest, I'm not sure what to do next. I suppose there was something very neat and reassuring about having my future planned out by my father. I've been looking in the newspaper at the jobs available, wondering what it is I might want to do. I'm not even sure which direction to take. My mother thinks it is very undignified for me to be looking to the newspaper for career options and has been discreetly asking at her bridge parties to see if anything "respectable" comes up.

No, I don't think it is very usual for women to go to college. There were female students at the University of Illinois but not many of them, especially not in biology. Even though they were attending college, they seemed to limit themselves to feminine courses of study, like modern languages, literature, home economics. Not a geologist among them, I'm afraid!

David

Isle of Skye
14 August 1913

Dear boy,

Why is it that things such as languages and literatures are "feminine" courses of study? No censure to you, David. I know you were repeating a universal truth—albeit a questionable one.

We are in an age where women work in professions previously prohibited. Although there still aren't many, women have proven themselves competent as doctors, scientists, business-women. Now that the doors are open, why aren't more women rushing to gain entrance? Instead, they are settling down, say-ing, "Who wants to win the Nobel Prize like Marie Curie? It will be much more satisfying to learn how to dress a roast chicken." Of course, everyone is welcome to their interests, and perhaps there are women who truly desire to learn nothing more than chicken-dressing or home economics. But why is a woman who has studied chemistry or geology less fit as a helpmeet than a woman who has studied literature? I'm not a suffragette, but when it comes to the topic of women and education, I do get irate.

Elspeth

Chicago, Illinois, U.S.A.
September 4, 1913

Dear Sue,

At long last, I am gainfully employed! I've got myself a job teaching biology and chemistry at a private school right here in Chicago. Lara says that, before the term is out, all of the girls will be in love with me and all of the boys will want to be my pals.

I don't have a good answer as to why some areas of study are designated as "feminine." You're right, we are moving into more-enlightened times, but are still far from there. With more co-educational universities, a woman can go to college and study what she pleases. She can even go ahead and find a "radical" new job, working as a scientist or an academic. But it is still assumed—even expected—that she will give it all up when she becomes a mother. Pedagogy and Equality are always trumped by Maternity.

Now, I will give you that women seem to be much better at raising children than men are. Lord knows, my father would've made a mess-up of the thing if he had been in charge. But children grow up, move away. Why shouldn't a woman be able to pursue a career later in life?

You make a good point, though, Sue. I hope for a wife who has more-interesting things to talk about than roasting chickens. Someone who reads the same things as I do and wonders about the same questions. Or even someone who thinks the exact opposite but doesn't mind lively debate and loves me just the same.

David

Isle of Skye
30 September 1913

David,

What, my dear boy, leads you to think that women are better at raising children? It sounds as though your niece adores you, so you must be doing something right with the child. Don't you have confidence in your ability to raise children, to care for them longer than it takes to tell a fairy story?

Elspeth

Chicago, Illinois, U.S.A.
October 17, 1913

Dear Sue,

Well, wouldn't you agree women have something innate, something that allows them to be mothers? I'm not quite sure what it is. Women are much more selfless than men. They have patience and a generous spirit. A woman could get all of the degrees in home economics she wishes, but even without having been to college, she can still run a household and become a mother.

David

Isle of Skye
31 October 1913

David,

Your letters have gone from merely rankling to downright infuriating. No innate quality makes us wives or mothers or homemakers. Are we born with something internal to make us good at cooking or darning socks? Do you think the Great Almighty had the foresight to know what would be required of the housewife of the twentieth century and reserve a special part of the brain for pie-making? Because, I tell you, I am proficient at none of those. No cooking, no pie-making, and certainly no darning of socks. Perhaps I was born with only half a brain, with something vital missing. Is that what you are suggesting?

You say that women, especially mothers, must be selfless.

They aren't born with this, yet it is still expected of them. No one begrudges a man his pint after a day's work or the chance to put his feet up in front of the fire or even the opportunity just to sit with the newspaper in the mornings. But if a mother wants to take an hour off for a walk, a quiet mug of tea, or (heaven forbid!) a visit to a friend's, there would be an outcry. Mothers aren't supposed to want to be away from their children. They are supposed to be completely selfless. A good mother would *never* eat the last slice of cake.

I'm not sure that I want children. I can't be that selfless. If I had a bairn clinging to my legs, I wouldn't be able to go on my jaunts through the mountains. I wouldn't be able to sit for hours staring at the waves, writing poetry. I wouldn't be able to get by with cooking only sausages and Christmas pudding. I couldn't stay up late, watching the stars move across the sky, or wake up early to walk the hills until the sun explodes over the horizon. You can't tell me that I could still have all of that with children in tow. And I could certainly never give up that last slice of cake.

Independence makes a woman greedy.

Elspeth

Chapter Six

~

Margaret

Edinburgh
Friday, 19 July 1940

Dear Paul,

She's gone.

The morning after the bomb fell, I went back to the house, intending to patch things up. All night, I couldn't sleep a wink, thinking about how we argued and how she pushed me away after those letters came tumbling out of the wall. My stomach was in knots.

But when I got up to the flat, it was empty. The wainscoting still gaped open, but every last letter was gone. And both of my suitcases.

My mother, who has never been away from the house for longer than a few hours, has packed up and left. And I have no idea where she's gone.

I went to the neighbours'. I checked in the library. I walked around Holyrood Park three times. I even stopped in St. Mary's Cathedral, thinking it not out of the realm of possibility that she was in her usual pew with the suitcases of letters. But no one had seen her. I went to Waverley Station, thinking surely she hadn't boarded a train, that she was just sitting on a bench, trying to work up the courage to board. No. She wasn't there.

So here I am, back in the empty house, not knowing if I should be worried or not. If she wants to take a little holiday, she's certainly entitled. She can take care of herself. But the way she looked last night, Paul. Her eyes, they were haunted. She looked defeated sprawled out there on the floor. I may not know where she is, but I know she's not on a jaunt to the seaside. Wherever she's gone, she's chasing something. Memories, regrets, her past. I'm not sure.

What I do know, though, is that it involves a letter from an American to someone named Sue. I always did like following a good mystery. Shall I?

> Affectionately,
> Margaret

21 July 1940

Maisie dear,

I hope this reaches you before you set out in search of adventure. You always did long to be a detective. Remember the time we crawled all over the Meadows at twilight, in search of the Hound of the Baskervilles? We were such kids then.

I do wish I had a bit of adventure myself. I'm still grounded until my wrist is all mended. So, instead of being off flying, I'm back lurking around the airfield. Can I be your Watson?

I hope, though, that your proposed detecting takes you safely out of Edinburgh. Granny never said a word about air raids in the city. Though, knowing her, she stood on the steps, shaking her fist at the Jerrys as they flew over. Now that I know there are real bombs falling right there where we used to play rounders, I hope you go elsewhere.

Perhaps your mam had the same thought. Don't worry about her, Maisie. She's as tough as my gran. She'll be just fine.

Be safe, my sweet lass.

> Yours,
> Paul

Edinburgh
Wednesday, 24 July 1940

Dear Paul,

I thought, if anyone I know could shed some light on Mother's "first volume," my cousin Emily could. She's known Mother longer than I have. I took that single yellowed letter to her house and, in between loads of washing at the steamie, she told me all she knew. Which, really, isn't much.

She remembers staying with Mother during the last war. Aunt Chrissie sent the children from the city to keep them safe after a Zeppelin attack. Even then there were evacuations. In their case, all the way up to the Isle of Skye.

I still can't believe that my mother, who's never walked beyond the edge of Edinburgh, once lived up in the Western Isles! It's no secret—she's told me stories of growing up, of skipping down the braes in search of fairy folk—but, nonetheless, I've always thought of her as an Edinburgher through and through. But she spent her girlhood there. Not so strange she should have a letter from Skye.

There was some bit of scandal with a girl and our two uncles. Perhaps the girl was called Sue? Emily couldn't remember. And I can't write to my gran to ask, as she only reads and writes in Gaelic. Emily suggested I write to our uncle Finlay, who stays in Glasgow.

I knew my mother had three brothers (two after Emily's da died), but she's never said much about them. Just that Alasdair was the smart one, Willie the cheeky one, and Finlay the one who lost something and never came back. About that, Mother never would explain further. Only that one day Finlay had more anger than he could keep inside and he left.

Emily never would've known Finlay was in the city at all— no one knew where he'd gone when he left Skye—but she was shopping in Glasgow one day years ago and passed a man who looked just like her da, Alasdair. She was young when he died, but Aunt Chrissie always kept a wedding photo by her bed. Emily chased the man down and, on a whim, threw out her da's name and was shocked to find out that he was Alasdair's younger brother. But it was no heartfelt meeting. Uncle Finlay shook her hand firmly, passed along his best wishes amidst other banalities, and then continued on his way. If Emily didn't immediately hurry to find a telephone directory and learn that he had an address in Glasgow, the family might have lost that one brief reappearance of Uncle Finlay.

Thank goodness for curiosity, else I'd probably not have the courage to write to an uncle I never knew existed. And a disagreeable uncle at that, if rumours are to be believed. Wish me luck!

Affectionately,

Margaret

Chapter Seven

~

Elspeth

Isle of Skye
5 November 1913

Davey,

I reread what I sent you last week, and I wanted to write again quickly, before you have a chance to respond. Although I still stand by everything I wrote in my earlier letter, I wish I had written a bit more gently.

I think you were wrong in what you said, about women having this mythical innate "motherness" inside. But, Davey, you're still young. I keep forgetting that. You've never been married, never had children of your own. You could very well feel this way for the rest of your life, but I can't hold you responsible for your beliefs right now. I'm sorry for expecting so much of you.

There! That's done. You should know that I don't often

apologise or recant words spoken in anger. And by "often," I mean "ever." I hope you're not *too* cross with me.

> Elspeth

Chicago, Illinois, U.S.A.
November 22, 1913

Dear Sue,

I wasn't sure how to respond, and so I'm glad you wrote again. I truly didn't mean to offend you. I don't have many women in my life. I have my mother and my sister, Evie, two of the most capable women I know. Evie couldn't wait for the day when her firstborn came into the world, and she just knew how to hold and feed Florence. And the other woman in my life, Lara, is counting down the days until she can get to running her own household. I swear, that girl has been dreaming about trousseaux and supper menus since she left the nursery.

You will be interested to know that I am officially an engaged man! I suppose as officially as one can be. I'd had poetically romantic notions about dropping on one knee and presenting a pearl set in gold, but Lara took one look at the ring and me and politely requested a band of diamonds. She loves to flash it around, as if to say, "He isn't a doctor, but we'll get by." No concrete plans yet for the wedding, but it will probably be a longer engagement. Lara has about two and a half years left before she graduates, and I wouldn't dream of adding the distraction of a wedding to her schoolwork. I can't count on anything modest or subtle, not with Lara and my mother planning it.

I suppose I should get my traveling in before the wedding, if I have only a few years left of bachelorhood. Perhaps I should come out to Oxford to visit Harry, the obliging friend who's been sending me your books. He's almost finished with his studies there, and I have a holiday coming up at the end of this term. Once that ring is on my finger, my traveling days may be over!

David

Isle of Skye
13 December 1913

David,

I'm so glad you aren't cross with me. You may find this funny, but I don't have many friends, at least not many who read poetry, ride cattle, or wear atrocious checked jackets. Why would you keep writing to a raving Scottish woman from some remote island in the Atlantic? At the risk of sounding horribly sentimental, I would quite miss your letters if they were to stop.

Officially engaged? My, my, but you are growing up, dear boy. Though perhaps I should lend you my rock-and-mineral guide, as you seem to have mistaken your Diamond for a Pearl.

I suppose we'll have to add commitment to the list of things you approach without fear, wild boy. What does scare you? Certainly not the college administration. Perhaps your father?

My fear at the moment is that I will run out of ink before I've finished this letter. Horrid old pen!

It will likely be after Christmas when this reaches you, but

I've made you one of my famous Christmas puddings (in miniature). Eat it in good cheer and have a marvellous holiday.

Elspeth

Chicago, Illinois, U.S.A.
January 12, 1914

A Happy New Year to you, Sue!

You're right, you *do* make a marvelous Christmas pudding! It's similar to the fruitcake my mother insists on making for us each Christmas. The woman doesn't set foot into the kitchen all year, unless it's to make a last-minute change to the menu. But every year, as the Christmas season approaches, she dons a lace-edged apron about as effective as a paper cake doily and waves all the staff out of the kitchen. Mother emerges hours later, hair floured, a smear of molasses on her cheek, and a shine in her eyes that could only be brought about by "sampling" the brandy, but victoriously bearing a fruitcake. It generally has the appearance, texture, and taste of a paving stone, but we must all eat a hearty slice on Christmas Eve.

The joy we had this year, Sue, was eating your delightful Christmas pudding. Both Evie and Hank insisted on examining the box you'd sent, to make sure I wasn't holding out on them. Even my father begged for more. When my mother asked, with the air of a jealous mistress, how this pudding compared to her fruitcake, we were quick to reassure her, "Oh, the Christmas pudding is good, but it's very . . . you know . . . *British*." We left it to her to interpret just what that meant.

Did you have a peaceful holiday? Any more kettles this year?
I regret to say that Santa Claus didn't leave a kettle for me, but I
did get a splendid new tennis racket. I can hardly wait until the
snow thaws to go try it out. Evie stitched a beautiful bookmark
that reads "A book is like a garden carried in the pocket." And
my father presented me with a watch, a gold number with a
thick chain. He told me it was his father's watch and his father's
before him. "Now that you're a man, David," says he, "and
have some direction in your life, you'll need something to help
guide you. You know *where* to go, but now you will know *when*
to go." The whole speech was rather stodgy, but Mother was
dabbing at her eyes and even Evie was sniffling. It's a handsome
watch but makes me think of my grandfather. I had been hoping
for a wristwatch, something I could wear while driving, climbing, and cycling, without looking as if I had just stepped out of
the nineteenth century.

My dad has been quite pleasant over the holidays. But I think
you might be right; if I have a fear, it would be my father.
I eventually did stand up to him about not going into medicine,
but if I hadn't done as poorly as I did my last semesters, I
wouldn't have had such an easy time of it. Even after all of his
talk about me "becoming a man," I still live under his roof, like
a child, obeying his rules. He doesn't approve of anything I do
or anyone I do it with.

I've always found it funny that my friend Harry is the one
person my dad *should* approve of but in actuality is the person
he disapproves of the most. Harry has to be one of my oldest
friends. We went to school together as children, pored over my
father's anatomy texts (more specifically poring over those

pages pertaining to the female anatomy), went on our first dates together under the philosophy of "safety in numbers." Harry's family moves in the same social circles, he's actually completing his medical studies, he's absolutely brilliant, and he's flawlessly polite. What could my father find fault with?

I suppose that a sharp mind can be wielded like any sharp weapon, and Harry can be quite disapproving of the snobbery he finds at many of the social functions we are forced to. He's lucky that most of the people he mocks don't catch his sarcasm and dry humor, or he wouldn't be invited back nearly so often. It's been quite a few years since Harry set off for Oxford. We write back and forth—not nearly as often as you and I write—but I'm looking forward to seeing him.

And a Christmas gift for you, dear Sue. A mottled black-and-pen, so that you'll always be able to write to me.

To a new year,
David

Isle of Skye
28 January 1914

Already 1914, and the world hasn't ended yet!

Davey, you misled me! This isn't a mottled pen at all. It's marbled through with red and black, just like a polished length of jasper. What better pen for a budding geologist?

I have a new set of chalks for Christmas, for drawing, but the rest of my gifts were unhappily practical—socks, three new

spoons, a giant washtub. Tennis racket? I've never played, but
it certainly sounds more exciting than a washtub.

Elspeth

Chicago, Illinois, U.S.A.
February 14, 1914

Dear Sue,

I've just gotten back from a ski trip to Ishpeming, Michigan,
with a few friends, which is why I'm a bit tardy in my response
to you. Not only was your letter waiting for me when I got
home, but I also had a letter from Harry. He's proposed that I
sail over to England, go on a sort of valedictory tour of Britain
with him, before sailing back to the States together. I don't
know the precise itinerary yet, but Harry is talking about heading up to Edinburgh in our rambles. This is probably a wild
idea, but, Sue, you should come to meet me! I know, a bit of a
lark, but you have until June to figure out a way to get yourself
on that ferry. May I suggest a great deal of whisky?

Happy Valentine's Day to you!

David

Isle of Skye
10 March 1914

David,

Are you completely mad? You think you'll be able to do
what all my family and friends have been unable to do? My
whole life, no one has been able to get me onto a boat. But you
think you'll succeed where others have failed? You think the
lure of David is greater than the lure of university? My, but you
are the cocky one!

    Elspeth

Chicago, Illinois, U.S.A.
March 26, 1914

Sue,

    You forget, my father is a doctor. I have ether.

    David

Isle of Skye
11 April 1914

My dear boy,

    Not nearly enough.

      E

Chicago, Illinois, U.S.A.
April 28, 1914

Dear Sue,

Plans are afoot! Itineraries are set, tickets are bought, rooms at the Langham in London booked, and I am ready to step on that boat. The question is, dear Sue, are you?

Surely you are just as curious as I am to see who is at the other end of that pen-and-paper. You're both scientist and artist, realist and dreamer. Curiosity is your middle name.

David

Isle of Skye
6 May 1914

Dear David,

Well, it's been awhile since I've seen my niece and nephews in Edinburgh. They would adore a visit from their auntie, wouldn't they?

I will expect that ether posted with your next letter. Buckets of it.

E

Chicago, Illinois, U.S.A.
May 21, 1914

Sue,

Be still my beating heart! Can it be true? Sue is going to
brave the ocean for me?

If all goes well, we should be arriving in Edinburgh on the
sixteenth. I know I won't be able to wait a moment longer than
that. The seventeenth at noon? St. Mary's Cathedral on York
Place?

> Crossing everything I've got,
> David

POST OFFICE TELEGRAPHS
SRP 5.55 EDINBURGH 25
18 JUNE 14

E. DUNN ISLE OF SKYE=
WAITED IN CATHEDRAL AS PLANNED WHERE ARE YOU
    PLEASE REPLY=
        DAVID CALEDONIAN HOTEL+

Liverpool, England, United Kingdom
June 22, 1914

What happened, Sue? I thought we had a deal. Did that ferry
prove too much for you? You're lucky I'm not one to hold a

grudge. But you do realize that, at the very least, you owe me an explanation! One that doesn't involve a ravaging water horse.

The trip has been great. Harry and I have had years to catch up on. He's not been the best of correspondents and, you may be surprised to hear, neither have I. You seem to inspire something special that makes me never run out of things to say.

Harry has got himself a sweetheart, Minna, a demure young lady who writes the most saccharine verse. I met her: very polite but quite flirtatious. She spent half the time discussing the weather and the price of tea in a precise, clipped accent and the other half trying to get Harry alone in the many corners of her parents' vast house. She's only eighteen, so no matter how much the rest of his anatomy was telling him otherwise, his head cooled long enough for him to decide not to pop the question just yet. He's heading back to the States to start medical school and a savings account. In the meantime, he hopes (although not *too* ardently!) that she develops at least one other skill or passion aside from trying to maneuver him into the bedroom at every opportunity. Harry's not holding his breath that Minna will be faithful, but we drank a toast to her trying anyway.

The cities we visited were lovely, but, truth to tell, I could've been back in Urbana and it would've been fine, as long as I was with Harry. Does that sound overly sentimental? He's started smoking a pipe and writing poetry (is *everyone* a poet these days?). Aside from that, he's the same old Harry, and we felt like little boys. I'm sure there were some occasions where we acted like little boys too.

We're getting ready to board the ship, but I wanted to write so I could mail this before I left Great Britain. I have a few more souvenirs to buy before we leave. I asked Florence what she wanted me to bring her back from my trip and she firmly requested an English pony. I don't think a pony would fit in my stateroom (that's what I get for sailing second class!), but how could I refuse the wishes of my favorite little girl?

Harry is going to send one more cable to Minna and has offered to drop this letter by the post office for me, so I'll close for now. I'll be looking for a letter full of fervent explanations and humble apologies from you! No more secrets, Sue!

David

Isle of Skye
3 July 1914

David,

I must say, I was amazed to get a letter from you so quickly; then I noticed you had mailed it from England, so it didn't have as far to go as usual.

You have every right to be angry at me, Davey. We had an agreement. Goodness, you traveled across an ocean to meet me. All I had to do was ferry across the sound.

What is my excuse, you may rightly ask? My old fear would be a handy one, for sure. But, alas, my fears in this case are sillier, perhaps even a bit more primitive. I'm afraid that, if we meet, the mystery will be gone. We might not get along the way we do on paper. What if our conversation doesn't flow like this in person?

You were waiting in St. Mary's Cathedral to meet an *ideal* of Elspeth Dunn. I didn't want you to be disappointed with the real thing. What if you thought I was too short? Or too old? Or you didn't like the sound of my voice? I just want to keep things the way they are, where I'm mysterious and, I hope, interesting.

I really did intend to come, though. Trust me in that, Davey.

As long as you think I'm keeping secrets, I have another one. But this one I'll keep close for a bit, for I know that you won't be able to stop laughing once you hear.

Harry sounds like a simply splendid friend. I would say that I hope to meet him someday, but I suppose I can't do that without meeting you—and we've already gone over that!

Elspeth

P.S. I truly hope that not everyone has become a poet, else I'll be out of a job!

Chicago, Illinois, U.S.A.
July 15, 1914

Sue, Sue, you funny thing. Did you never stop to think that perhaps I worried about the same "what-ifs"? Avoiding a face-to-face meeting was to my advantage. You wouldn't see how big my feet are or how clumsy I am when off the dance floor. I think you have a good opinion of me now (aside from my taste in jackets, I suppose). After all, I'm devilishly handsome. Wickedly clever. Witty and utterly brilliant. Why would I want to jeopardize that? All those illusions could vanish the moment we said hello. But for the elusive chance to meet you . . . all of those apprehensions pale in comparison.

We've been writing for, what, two years now? (I say that with a bit of nonchalance, as though I haven't saved every letter you've ever sent.) Really, can there still be mystery after all of that time? We've told our deepest fears, confessed our secret longings. I *know* you, Sue, and I think you know me too. If I were sitting in front of you, saying this right now, I should hope my words wouldn't mean less just because you disliked the sound of my Midwestern accent.

Think about when you first meet a person, Sue. You have to get past all the superficial nonsense, the appraisals of accents and checked jackets. An interrogation of appearance. After you've deemed each other worthy, then you can actually settle down to get acquainted, to begin those first tentative probes of the mind. Find out what sort of thing fuels the other—what makes them scream, what makes them laugh, what makes them tremble on the rug. You and I are lucky. We never had to worry about the first part, the visual sizing up. We got to go directly to the interesting bit. The getting to know the depths and breadths of each other's soul.

I don't know about you, but I find it refreshing. I am sick to death of having to worry whether people think I look old enough or respectable enough or whatnot. Always having to be polite and look interested. When I write to you, I don't have to think about any of that nonsense. I don't have to worry about my big feet. I can peel away the husk (if you will forgive a corn metaphor) and reveal the shiny kernels of my dreams and passions and fears. They are yours, Sue, yours to gnaw on as you will! Marvelous with a sprinkle of salt.

Now, after all that, you *must* tell me your new secret. I can promise that I won't laugh. At least not loud enough that you could hear me from Chicago. . . .

I'm starting to nod off and so pulled out my watch. I'm not going to admit to how early in the morning it is, but the streets have long been quiet. I hope you're sleeping a bit more soundly than I am right now!

David

Isle of Skye
18 August 1914

Davey,

What is the world coming to?

Eight weeks ago, I stood on the pier, trying to find the nerve to step on that ferry. I kept my eyes on that horizon, knowing that if I went to meet it, to meet you, everything would change. Not necessarily in the going, but in the leaving. Women like me don't go across the water to rendezvous with fascinating Americans. They wait at home for their husbands' boats to return.

So I went back to my cottage, to reread your letters and pretend I didn't almost get on that ferry. To wait for Iain to return from chasing the herring up the Minch. To think of a way to tell him that, after so many years, I was pregnant.

The day he came home, I was out hanging the wash in the garden, ankle-deep in mud. He stepped through the gate, dropped his seabag, and said grimly, "We're at war."

Everything felt so cold, Davey, my news forgotten. I asked who he meant by "we," but he just handed me a newspaper.

Four days before, Great Britain declared war on Germany. While I had sat alone in my cottage, reading through old letters and fortifying my heart, the world went to war.

He said he was joining up as soon as he could pack. He'd only just come home and he was leaving again. And for what? What makes him think this war has anything to do with him? With our island? With *us*? "Our world has already vanished," he said. "I can't get it back, but I'll sure as hell try to keep the rest from going to pieces."

He was so *calm*, Davey. I remember looking over his shoulder while he was talking and noticing a gull flying, as if in slow motion. Even the sheep quieted. The whole island slowing down to listen to his pronouncement. As if it made sense! And I felt a pain deep inside; I was sure it was the proverbial "heart breaking."

Later that day I found that I had lost the bairn I'd been carrying. A bairn unasked for, but, truly, not unwanted. I'd had time to grow accustomed to the idea, but now, gone, with just a feeling of emptiness left behind. Perhaps I was right all along. Perhaps the universe never meant for me to be a mother. Just like that, I lost my husband, my child, and the peaceful world I had known. The next week, Iain marched off with Finlay and the other Territorials for training.

Oh, Davey, I need a letter from you. I need a kind word, I need a funny word, I need a picture of you in a silly checked jacket. I need to forget that all this is happening.

Elspeth

Chapter Eight

~

Margaret

Edinburgh
Wednesday, 24 July 1940

Dear Sir,

I apologise for this unexpected letter. I'm not even sure that I am writing to the right Finlay Macdonald.

I have reason to believe that you may be my uncle. My mother is Elspeth Dunn, once of Skye, currently of Edinburgh. My cousin Emily Macdonald (Alasdair's daughter) passed this address on to me after meeting you once in Glasgow. I have never met either of my uncles, and I would like to become better acquainted.

May I write to you?

Sincerely,

Margaret Dunn

Glasgow
25 July

Margaret,
    Haven't you already done that?
       Finlay Macdonald

27 July 1940

Dear Maisie,
    I'm airborne again! And not a moment too soon. We're
being hit all over the place down here in the south. I was really
chafing being on the ground. How is it up in Edinburgh?
    Have you sent the letter to your uncle? Any reply yet?
       Love,
       Paul

Edinburgh
Monday, 29 July 1940

Dear Paul,
    He wrote. In a way. And, I suppose, by not disagreeing
with me or *completely* disregarding me, he's confirmed that, yes,
he is indeed the Finlay Macdonald in question. When I asked
if I may write to him, his only response was, "Haven't you
already done that?" Truly, he must be my uncle. He has Mother's prickly wit.

I won't write back to him. I'd be weighing each and every word to be absolutely sure he wouldn't make fun of it. And that's far too much work. Why couldn't I have a long-lost uncle who declares me his sole heir or bestows upon me his priceless collection of artefacts from the South Seas, as in the books? Or, at the very least, inhabits an insane asylum. I'm sure I read a story like that once. Insane asylum, I think I could stomach. But a stinging reply? I think not.

 Margaret

P.S. Don't ask about Edinburgh. A 1,000-pound bomb on Albert Dock, incendiaries all along the railway lines and in Granton. If Mother were here, she'd be a wreck. And now I have to worry about you too. Please be careful.

31 July 1940

Dear Maisie,

 Where's that sense of adventure I love so much? Where's that curiosity to see what's beyond the next peak, the willingness to hurtle headlong into any situation if it means it may make you breathless for at least a moment? I always say to the other lads around here that, if my fiancée were a man, she'd give them all a run for their money up here in the air.

 Don't you worry about me for a single second. I keep a snapshot of you in my pocket, and, when I look upon your bonny eyes, that's all the luck I need.

 You do realise, his reluctance to write you a proper reply

hints at an even better story. Come, Watson, come! The game is afoot!

> Love,
> Paul

Edinburgh
Friday, 2 August 1940

Dear Paul,

I'll do it. For you. But only for you.
> Maisie

Edinburgh
Friday, 2 August 1940

Dear Sir,

Or should I say "Uncle Finlay"?

I must admit to being puzzled by your reply. Was it a dismissal? Discouragement? Tacit permission to write again?

Please, I have so many questions about my mother, things she's never told me. You don't have to join me for tea or come to my wedding. Just a few moments of your time to write and tell me about my mother. Help me fill in the blanks from the "first volume" of her life.

> Appreciatively,
> Margaret Dunn

Glasgow
3 August

Margaret,

Have you considered that your mother has kept that book closed for a reason?

Have you also considered that a man alone may just want to be left alone?

Really, I have nothing to say about Elspeth that you'd want to hear. Sometimes not even years can erase disappointment.

Finlay Macdonald

Edinburgh
Monday, 5 August 1940

Dear Uncle Finlay,

I don't mean to sprinkle salt on old wounds. Truly, I don't. I don't wish to pry into your personal business. I just want to know my mother better. And I believe you're just as curious about her *now* as I am about her *then*, else you wouldn't have replied. Twice.

So, to repay your anticipated kindness, I'll tell you something about my mother every time you tell me something. Tit for tat.

Sincerely,

Margaret Dunn

Glasgow
6 August

Margaret,

Tit for tat. In the trenches, we used to call that "live and let live." If the Boche did not fire, we did not fire. We left them a few moments of peace at times, and they left us with a wee bit of peace in return. Of course, Command didn't agree with this. They told us to fire first, to keep the enemy on edge. To convince them to leave us alone.

You are a stubborn lass. I'll give you that. Just like Elspeth. She was as stubborn as they come, though, in a house of three boys, I suppose she had to be.

Tit for tat. I never did think Command had it right.

Finlay Macdonald

Chapter Nine

~

Elspeth

Chicago, Illinois, U.S.A.
September 10, 1914

Dear Sue,

I really wish I knew a good joke or an amusing story to tell
you.

Have you heard from your husband? Do you know yet if he
is being sent overseas? At least you can rest assured that you are
safe up on Skye. I'm thankful for that.

And, Sue, it's probably a breach of etiquette to say so, but
my heart breaks to hear that you lost a baby. I wish I knew the
right words, but know that I hold them in my heart.

I don't have any more photos of me in my checked jacket,
but I promise the next time I buy a ridiculous-looking coat, you
will be the first person I send a picture to. I'm almost tempted to
go out and buy one just for you, if it'll make you smile.

You know, you've never mentioned your husband before.
I suppose I knew you were married, being a "Mrs." and all, but
you've never talked about him. Funny, since we've talked about
pretty much everything else.

Please keep me updated. I can read the reports in the newspaper, but, from way across the ocean, it's hard to know what is
really happening over there.

I'm here for you,
David

Isle of Skye
4 October 1914

David,

Well, I've finally heard from Iain. His battalion is at a training camp in Bedford. He expects they'll get called up any day,
but I imagine most men say that. What else do they have aside
from anticipation? It was a short letter, talking cheerfully of
training and weapons and how they all hope to "get a few
Huns." Not a word of me or our home or the bairn I'd lost.

My brother Finlay enlisted too, at the same time as Iain.
Those two were inseparable growing up. It only stood to reason
they'd go off to war together. My mother refuses to let my
youngest brother, Willie, join up. He's her baby, and she'll hold
him close for as long as she can. Willie's been going about in a
black cloud since Finlay went off. I think Màthair's made a mistake and let the wrong one go. Willie's always her lad, but Finlay, once he's had a taste of the world, might never want to

come back. He's not made to be a crofter or a fisherman. I think the only thing that will bring him back to Skye is Kate.

I've been trying to write, to go out walking by myself and compose some poems. But they all come out jumbled. Not quite right. I need things back to normal. I need to keep my mind from things. I can't think about Iain or Finlay or any of our other boys getting ready to go off to fight and die.

I'm not sure why I didn't tell you about my husband. I suppose it just never fit into our conversations. But now I'm weary of not always telling you the absolute truth.

Elspeth

Chicago, Illinois, U.S.A.
November 2, 1914

Dear Sue,

I can understand how your brother Willie feels. You know me, I wouldn't be happy either if I were left behind while everyone else went off to war. I'd want the adventure too.

I know it may not be much, but I've started writing down those fairy stories I've been telling Florence. I've included one with this letter—"The Mouse King's Cheese." Florence adores cheese! I thought you might find it entertaining, something to pass the time. It's not finished, though. I'm not quite sure how to end it. Maybe you have an idea?

Another term has begun and I feel a bit more confident, having taught these classes all before. We've just finished talking about the history of chemistry (starting from the alchemists, then Lavoisier, Mendeleev, and the like). My students turned in the most appalling set of essays. To think, they will be the next generation of statesmen and lawyers, and they can't even construct a proper argument! At any rate, when I was reading these and ruminating that I (I hope!) wrote a bit better at that age, I couldn't help but think of you.

Sue, you must start writing again. Don't try to force yourself, but tuck a pencil and a square of paper in your waistband, so that whenever and wherever your muse returns to you, you will be able to stop and scribble it down. Emerson said, "Genius is the activity which repairs the decay of things," and he was talking about poetry. I think if you get to writing again, that could be the thing to help you return to the normality that you crave.

In any case, don't stop writing to me, no matter what. It may not be poetry to you, but I've never thought of your letters as anything less.

Waiting for the poetry,
David

Isle of Skye
29 November 1914

Dear David,
Oh, I think the horrid little girl should stay a mouse forever! Climbing onto the table to reach the bread on the other side? I do hope your niece has nicer table manners than that.

Well, if you can't leave Lottie as a mouse, what could you do to her? I mean aside from having her be caught by Mrs. Owl and made into mouse mousse. She has to learn her lesson somehow. Maybe something involving the pies cooling on her mother's window? (O, what a temptation. . . .) Or maybe she has to rescue the Mouse King in some way and thus receives his undying gratitude? Maybe she falls in love with the Mouse King? I don't know for certain, but someone in a gold velvet robe and miniature shoes has to be quite eye-catching. As though he were wearing a checked jacket. It wouldn't be surprising if she fell in love.

You'll be pleased to know I've dashed off a few poems. I took your advice and began to carry my notebook and pencil along with me, and one morning, as I was washing the floor (how mundane these things are sometimes!), an idea came to me. I sat there on the wet floor while my wash water cooled, and I jotted down a poem. It isn't the "genius" of Emerson, but it seemed to capture my thoughts at the moment.

I've had to take over many of Iain's chores now that he's left. Yesterday the wind snapped one of the ropes we use to secure the thatch on the roof. A patch worked its way loose during the night, and I was greeted with a pile of snow in my kitchen come morning. You should've seen me on the roof, clinging on with one hand like one of Kipling's Bandar-Log, trying to tie down a bundle of thatch with the other. When I came in, my eyebrows and eyelashes were all frozen together, and I had to suck on my fingers in order to thaw them enough to make a cup of tea. I've taken to wearing my trousers nearly every day, such is the work that I've been doing. I know that Iain didn't think of that when he decided to up and leave to follow boyish dreams of glory.

You know, Davey, the nights are the worst. I sit by the fire, knitting or holding an unread book on my lap, and I can't stop my mind from racing, can't stop my ears from hearing every rattle and creak. I try to go to bed early, so that I don't have to think and feel alone, but I just can't fall asleep. I admit, I've been pulling out all of your old letters and rereading them, sometimes falling asleep covered in your words. It makes me feel that you are really here and that I'm not alone. I can imagine we're talking. Absurd, I know, since we've never actually talked and I don't know what your voice sounds like. By the way, do you realise how *pretentious* you sounded in your early letters to me? You must have really wished to impress me.

I finally feel tired, so I think I'll end this now and blow out the candle. If the weather holds tomorrow, I'll be able to post this, but I think the mail is taking longer these days.

Elspeth

Terre Haute, Indiana, U.S.A.
December 23, 1914

Dear Sue,

I'm in Terre Haute, spending Christmas with Evie, Hank, and Florence. I got your letter as I was leaving for the station and was happy to have such pleasant reading material for the train. Such a lengthy missive; the winter nights on Skye must be long indeed.

Your suggestions roused me to finish "The Mouse King's Cheese," so I now include the ending of this story for your perusal (approval?). I've read the completed tale to Florence, who jumped up and down and cried, " 'Gain! Read it 'gain!" If I can inspire a similar response in you, I will be satisfied.

I'm surprised to hear you refer to "boyish dreams of glory," you who are always so careful to avoid labeling based on gender. Around here, I hear as many women as men berate President Wilson for keeping America's toes neatly out of the maelstrom in Europe. America hasn't had a war in a while; we're spoiling for a fight.

Just last night at dinner Evie got into quite a tirade against Wilson. Our grandfather fought near the end of the Civil War, and we grew up listening to his stories. That man could spin a tale! No one else could make war sound so unlike war. He enthralled even young Evie, such that she pasted on a fake mustache and played Rough Riders with me all summer.

Even though Dad didn't have a war when he was in the prime of his life, he stayed out of the army, to his father's eternal disappointment. Not sure Gramps ever forgave him for that. He thought soldiering and war a civic duty; Dad thought it suicide. If America jumps into the fight, I may join up simply to spite Dad.

But cheerier thoughts certainly are needed. Evie has already been spoiling the festivities here with talk of war. Hank is ready to send her to sleep in the barn. The merriest of Christmases to you, Sue. You may be quite alone there in your little cottage, but know that you are not forgotten and that someone is thinking of you this Christmas.

David

Isle of Skye
21 January 1915

Dear Davey,

A new year and a belated Christmas gift for you. My newest book! Your letter and the box of freshly printed books from my publisher arrived on the same day, so you will receive one of the very first copies. It seems so strange to read these poems now, as they were all written before the war. So different from the themes of my recent poetry. No flowers, clouds, and summer days. I'm writing on darker subjects and emotions now: loneliness, anger, bleak winters. I'm not sure it's that good, but at least it is helping to "slay my dragons," as they say.

I get news so sporadically from Iain that I may go mad. Really, I hear more about him from Finlay. Thank goodness for a letter-writing brother. In fact, I think I may already be going mad, as I'm considering moving into my parents' cottage until Iain comes home. I slipped on some ice and sprained my ankle the other day whilst out walking. Luckily, I was in town buying groceries at the time and someone was able to get me to the doctor's, but it made me worry. What if it had happened when I was at home alone? I don't have a telephone and I would've been quite by myself, unless someone happened by for an unexpected visit.

I'm also fed up with all of the tasks around here. A croft is hard enough to run with a whole family helping out, but a single person? Everything seems to be falling apart on me. Another rope snapped on the roof. I climbed up again and realised that all of the ropes are weak. I don't know if they're shot

through with mould, if the birds have got them, or if it's a problem with my plaiting, but they are fraying and pulling apart.
I ask you, Davey, what is a well-published poet doing scrambling onto a thatched roof in the dead of winter, a length of heather rope between her teeth? Shouldn't I be somewhere in a leather armchair in front of a roaring library fire? Would you be there too?

I enjoyed the ending to "The Mouse King's Cheese." Lottie grows up, she learns to share and say "thank you." I still think it would have been splendid if she had fallen in love with the Mouse King, checked jacket and all. What did Lara think of this story?

      Take care,
      Elspeth

Chicago, Illinois, U.S.A.
February 16, 1915

Dear Sue,

You'll never believe, but I sent one of my fairy stories to a magazine! I don't expect a reply for some time, but I thought you'd be proud to know I screwed up the courage to get "The Fairies' Twilight Ball" out there. Without your encouragement, I never would've even written the stories down. What made you decide to send out your poetry the very first time?

Your new book is marvelous! And you've even autographed it for me. I rate as a "dear friend" now? I can see what you mean about the lightness of the themes (of course, I haven't

read anything that you've been writing recently), but perhaps
we all need to read about flowers, clouds, and summer days in
these times.

I'm back at school now after the holiday. I've been bringing
in newspapers for my students to read. I've found them to be
woefully uninformed about what is going on in Europe. If Wilson lets us into the war, some of my senior students could enlist.
At least now they no longer think that the Balkans are somewhere near Sweden.

To answer your question, I don't know what Lara thinks of
"The Mouse King's Cheese." She hasn't read any of my stories.
To be perfectly honest, I'm not sure what it is that she reads.
I've tried to lend her some of my favorites, but she passes them
back as "boys' books." All I catch her reading these days are
fashion magazines and guest lists as we plan for the wedding.
After then, she should have more time to settle back with a
book. Right?

I wish you luck on moving in with your parents. You are a
brave woman! Over here, I'm looking forward to just the opposite.

David

Isle of Skye
8 March 1915

Dear David,

Soon after to writing you, I received a letter from Iain, saying they were being sent to the front at last and would be leaving on Friday. Of course, it was Friday morning when I got the letter, so they were already gone.

Why couldn't he send a telegram? Maybe I would have been able to work up the courage to get on that ferry, to see my husband one more time. I haven't seen him since just after war was declared, more than half a year ago. I know he's had leave in that time, as Finlay has been home to visit. But when I asked him about it, he said he certainly didn't have enough money to make the trip all the way from Bedford. He's infuriating! I have a modest amount put away from the sales of my books, but Iain stubbornly refuses to touch a penny. All he had to do was leave his obstinacy in his kit bag and let me buy him a ticket to come say goodbye. Now he's at the front, and who knows if I will see him again?

I'm doing well, aside from all of that. We're not as hard hit on Skye as in the big cities. My brother's widow, Chrissie, is in Edinburgh, and she writes of how scarce some foodstuffs are becoming. At least we have our own produce and as much milk as our cows will give. This time of year is always a bit tougher, when we're hoping for some fresh greens and soft fruit. But I still have a good stock of neeps, swedes, tatties, and smoked fish, so I can't complain. I am running low on tea, though, and have been reusing my leaves when I can. Sugar has gone up in price, but it's not as though I'm making marzipan cakes or sugar biscuits these days.

So Iain is in France and, beyond that, I don't know what is happening. I just pray that he and Finlay will keep an eye on each other, the way they always have. I pray they will stay safe.

Elspeth

Chicago, Illinois, U.S.A.
March 29, 1915

I hardly know what to say. I'm trying to put myself in your shoes, in your frame of mind, so that I can empathize as well as sympathize. I simply can't do it. I'm sorry.

I really should be brushing off my morning coat and practicing my speech, as the wedding isn't far off. And what am I doing instead? Sitting at my desk, writing to you, Sue. I know I should be more excited about the upcoming nuptials, but I suppose it is natural to feel a bit of apprehension. Not that I doubt my decision . . . but I'm feeling a little anxious about the whole event. Lara is excited enough for the both of us. She seems to be all wrapped up in dress fittings and whispered conferences with her friends.

I don't know all of the plans being concocted, only that everyone we've ever met or could ever hope to meet will be there. We'll probably serve platters of hors d'oeuvres that will go back to the kitchen mostly untouched and then twice as much roast meat as our guests could hope to eat. The women will all be dressed too elegantly and laced too tightly to do more than nibble on the food. This will be washed down with enough champagne to fill several bathtubs—the only part of the feast the guests will consume enthusiastically—and followed by a course of cakes and pastries so sweet they would make a dentist weep. After all this, I still have the honeymoon.

And I can't help but think of you, Sue, sitting alone by the fire in your cottage, "making do" with salted fish and potatoes, weak tea and unsweetened cake. I do admit to feeling a twinge of guilt; all of my extravagant feasting and leisure when you and the boys at the front are doing so much but getting so little in return. If someone were to ask where I would rather be on my wedding day—in a room full of strangers, trying to consume my portion of the feast, or alone in a cottage with you, Sue, drinking weak tea—I know which I'd choose.

David

Isle of Skye
17 April 1915

David,

Well, I've moved into my parents' cottage. It's getting to be too much living by myself, in more ways than one. I was spending nearly every day at the post office, waiting for word, but I realised how pathetic that was. Bad news will find you, no matter how far you run.

Also, it was too hard for me to maintain the cottage. I've made a bold decision, though, to have a new cottage built, a modern stone building with a slate roof and a chimney. I have Iain's separation allowance and he isn't here to tell me I can't. I've hired joiners and everything. Here's a wee sketch of what I'm planning. I'm going to leave the old blackhouse up for the animals. No more sharing my cottage with the hens!

I haven't heard from Iain in quite some time. If it weren't so grim, I would laugh, as I get more mail from a man I've never met than I do from my own husband. But, as they say, no news is good news.

I know I didn't say it in my last letter, but I *am* proud that you've sent one of your fairy stories off to a magazine. Have you heard anything yet? Please let me know how it goes.

You asked how I worked up the courage to send off my poetry. It was Finlay. Growing up, the two of us were never content. We'd sit on the beach, he carving, and me either sketching or scribbling. Our eyes on the horizon, no words were needed. But then he grew old enough for Da to take him on the boat. He'd go off fishing and leave me behind on the shore. He always brought me back stones he found, so that I'd feel I was with him. But I knew that, though he sailed away most mornings, it wasn't an escape. Sure as anything, going out on the boats tied him to the island. He'd never be able to leave. And so he made me promise to send out my poems, to try to send something of myself out into the world. Because he, he was trapped. But the rest of the world was mine for the taking.

I broke into the schoolhouse every night for a week to use the headmistress's prized typewriter, pecking away until I had a pile of poems typed to send. In this instance, crime did pay. The rest is, as they say, history! If you can believe it, I was only seventeen.

My publisher has been amazingly patient with me and my reclusion, but he sent me the most curious letter last week. Ages ago, he had asked for a photograph of me, to be included in the frontispiece of one of the books. He's finally said that, since I do not have a photograph to send him, he will send a photographer to me! I am waiting to hear a final confirmation, but I believe he is coming in a couple of weeks. I can't tell you how nervous I am, Davey! I've never had my photo taken before; I've never seen myself through someone else's eyes (or lens, as it were). I have no idea what to wear. We don't want the world to be disappointed at the one and only photograph of Elspeth Dunn.

At some point you are going to have to make a decision one way or another about the wedding, dear one. You need to decide if you want to be on the ferry when it sets off or if you are happier back on the sturdy pier. I know that you are not a man content to wait behind and just watch as the ferry chugs away. But perhaps this isn't your boat. Perhaps it doesn't sail where you want to go. You'll make the right decision. I think you already know what it is.

E

Chicago, Illinois, U.S.A.
May 9, 1915

Dear Sue,

You sound like you are doing well, despite not knowing what is happening at the front. Who knows, I may be able to give you a firsthand account if Wilson finally gives in. After the *Lusitania*, everyone here is howling for German blood. Twelve hundred people who had nothing to do with this war died on that ship. What was it you said in your first letter? We're all cowboys and outlaws here in the United States. If we get over there, the kaiser had better watch out!

The term is winding down and I hope that my students are leaving my classroom slightly better for it. Many still dismiss the war as a European problem, but a fair number see that it's big-

ger. Gone are the days when our countries are isolated. This is
the twentieth century. What affects one country affects us all.
Now my students see that the world is worth fighting for.

You really screwed up the courage to send off your poetry
when only seventeen? Sue, you're amazing! And, if you don't
mind me doing the math, younger than I thought for someone
so obviously distinguished. Seventeen when you started and,
checking the date in the front of your first book, only twenty-
seven now. You tease about being "old," but there are only four
years between us.

I hope that your photo sitting went well, if it's happened yet,
and that you weren't resigned to wearing your old trousers or
being photographed among the sheep. I should dearly like to see
the result.

David

Isle of Skye
29 May 1915

Oh, Davey, this foolish, foolish war!

There was a great battle at Festubert. The battalion that most
of our Skye boys are in was front and centre. Almost every family I know here lost a son or husband or father to the hungry
maw of this war at that single battle.

My brother Finlay, he was wounded quite badly. A shell fell
just in front of him, thankfully missing him but tearing open his
left leg with fragments. He was quite literally one step away
from disaster. Màthair's gone to see him—he's earned himself a

"Blighty," as the English say, and is in hospital down in London. I actually followed her down to the pier and was a hairbreadth away from getting on that ferry. But I couldn't. Not even for Finlay. I cried into my sleeve for being gutless, then wrote him a poem on my handkerchief. I hope it will say what I cannot. I hope he'll know how much I love him. I'm waiting up here on Skye for Màthair to write, praying it's not as bad as I imagine.

Iain was wounded too, but not badly enough that he was out of the trenches for more than a few days. He didn't even write to me, just sent a pre-printed Field Service postcard, where you cross off the lines that don't apply, giving a staccato message: "I have been admitted into hospital / wounded / and am going on well." A letter from him followed, a short note saying he was fine—just a nick in the shoulder, nothing to worry about—but could I send some cigarettes?

And do you know what's strange, Davey? I'm really not worried, at least about Iain. I feel a bit hollow. I feel lonely, but that's not an unusual feeling these days. I feel somehow wistful, though for what I'm not sure. But I don't feel sad or angry or scared or worried. At least not right now.

I pray that America doesn't get involved in this. Stay right where you are, Davey. Don't give in to the taunts of a bully. I don't want a reason to *start* worrying.

> Praying,
> Elspeth

Chicago, Illinois, U.S.A.
June 15, 1915

Dear Sue,

Why is it that I'm always at a loss for words when you need them the most? If my thoughts of you right now could be put into words so easily, then you would be getting the firmest of epistolary embraces. How is Finlay?

The disorder in Europe seems to mirror the disorder in my own life. First, Evie's husband is ill. It didn't seem very serious at first, but he has taken quite a long time to recover. Florence is staying at my parents' house now. You can imagine how nervous Evie is about Florence's health. The moment Hank felt the least bit feverish, she sent Florence away.

I've postponed the wedding. Lara's furious. I told her it wasn't fitting to go ahead with the festivities, not with Hank so sick. I don't think she believed it was my only reason. Truth is, I don't either. Perhaps you're right. Perhaps this just isn't my ferry. Though I don't expect her to be content with that.

Don't they say bad luck comes in threes? If Hank's illness is the first, and my canceled wedding the second, then the third has to be that I was asked to not come back to my teaching position next year. They were very polite about it, but, essentially, I was canned. It seems the parents took issue with me bringing in newspapers, telling my students about the *Lusitania* and other atrocities. Mommy and Daddy didn't want their precious darlings to know what a horrible place the world really is. Here I am, trying to educate, and I get sacked for doing it too well. "Stick to the periodic table," I was told.

And no such luck with "The Fairies' Twilight Ball." The magazine sent it back with an impersonal note saying that it didn't fit their needs and they "regretfully decline." A rejection is a rejection. So, you see, I'm failing all around.

But I suppose nothing was ever accomplished without a little perseverance. I'll reschedule the wedding, start scanning the want ads again, send out my story to yet another magazine. I wouldn't be "Mort" if I shied away from a bit of a challenge. I fell off the drainpipe and broke my leg, but, you know, I was up that same drainpipe just a few months after that little event.

One of the good things I've got going for me is that I've finally left my parents' house. Harry rented an apartment after coming back to the States and I've moved in with him. It's like being in England with him all over again.

The other good thing in my life is you.

I hope things are going better for you now, dear Sue.

Thinking of you,
David

Isle of Skye
2 July 1915

Dear David,

Finlay's lost his leg. Only below the knee, but that's more than anyone wants to lose. He couldn't work up the nerve to tell Màthair in his letter. Of course, she doesn't care. She's just thanking God he's alive. We all are. He's been moved to hospital in Edinburgh for recovery and therapy and will be back on

Skye after he's fitted for a prosthetic. We won't be able to take
the rambles we used to, but at least I'll have my brother back.

I was getting quite worried as I read through your letter, as
you sounded so earnest. So much happening to you, enough to
get even the most stouthearted person down. I was much relieved to hear you admit you were still the same old "Mort," the
boy who could climb a drainpipe with a sack full of squirrels
and a heart full of merriment. I think if my Davey wasn't cheerful and laughing in the teeth of danger, then nothing would be
right in the world. How do you think I've been able to keep my
spirits up through all of this? How do you think I've been able
to stay afloat in this sea of chaos?

The picture-taking went well. Before Màthair left London, I
sent her a postal order and begged her to buy me a dress, something nice and modern. I must have sent far too much, for she
brought back a sensible brown wool suit and blouse, a completely pragmatic dress (grey like the Scottish skies in winter),
and an utterly frivolous rose-coloured gown. The rose dress is a
fluttery, flimsy affair and seems terribly immodest after the great
lumpy things I was wearing before, but it feels like I'm wearing
a rainbow and it makes me look years younger, as if I never had
things like wars to worry about.

The photographer convinced me to wear the rose-coloured
dress, saying it made me look more like a poet—"ethereal" was
the word he used. Naturally he wanted to get a picture outside,
against the backdrop of which I write, so he posed me by the
garden, down on the shingle, and, yes, Davey, even by the
sheep. I felt quite silly, for what Highland girl wears an insub-
stantial little feather of a dress to go out herding sheep or climb-

ing hills? But I shouldn't complain, as the pictures came out rather well. You can't even see that I have on my old black boots underneath. My mother keeps a small flower garden, and I think the pictures taken there turned out the best. It was quite curious to see my own face in a photograph. I have never seen myself in such a detached way before. The photographer sent me a few prints of my own, so here you go. Now you can see what I really look like. I hope you aren't disappointed.

Last night I sat outside the cottage, watching the moon rise, notebook and pencil on my lap. The garden smelled like foxglove and honeysuckle, with, of course, the tangy scent of the sea. It was even cool enough that I wasn't bothered much by the midges. Màthair brought me out a Thermos flask of tea before she went to bed. I stayed out all night. I had my hot tea and my notebook. Who could want for anything more? The night seemed so pregnant, so poignant, one of those Scottish nights that make you understand why some still believe in spirits and wee folk. I was expectant, waiting out there for something I'm not sure I found. When my da came out to do the milking in the morning, he found me fast asleep on the bench beside the house, "all covered in dew like a fairy," he said. Now you can see where I get my poetry!

You know, I'm content right now, but that contentment is as fragile as an egg. I'm cushioning it and trying to keep it from the booms and crashes across the channel. I'm so afraid something is going to crash so loud that it will reach clear across to my little island.

    E

Chicago, Illinois, U.S.A.
July 21, 1915

Dear Sue,

I have your picture propped up on my desk as I'm writing this, and I'm trying to imagine you reading my letter after it arrives. Your description—it didn't do you justice. I don't think I need to tell you how lovely you look to me.

But now, having seen your picture, I can see why your dad thought you looked like a fairy asleep in the garden. If I wasn't certain you were bigger than my thumb, I should've guessed your dress was fashioned from rose petals and spiders' webs. You look quite fey amid the blooms. And your expression is so wistful. What were you thinking of right then when the photo was snapped?

I didn't realize the stories of my antics and asinine exploits were so important to you—"afloat in this sea of chaos"? I never hoped I could achieve more than a hearty chuckle or round of applause for the stunts I pull. I feel I have a lot to live up to now, but, as always, I'm up to the challenge. If you believe—

Since writing the above, something has happened. Harry let Lara into my room to surprise me and she spotted the letter on my desk. She snatched it and read it before I realized what was happening. Lara's called the engagement off for good, in fact tossed the engagement ring in my wastebasket. She says she fancies I'm in love with you and she can't compete with someone who's been winning all along.

You know, for a girl who didn't finish college, she's quite smart.

David

Isle of Skye
4 August 1915

Davey, oh, Davey! You shouldn't have written what you did. If you hadn't written it, then I wouldn't be in this quandary. I could go along, carrying my secrets. I would go on expecting to be a widow, checking the newspapers to see each fresh casualty list. You would go on being my cheerful correspondent, an admirer of my poetry, and an interesting friend. And now you've spoiled that with your last letter. You can never now be just my "interesting friend."

What *should* I say? I *should* say that it's terribly presumptuous of you to write to a married woman and claim to be in love with her. But what do I *wish to* say? I *wish to* say that I don't think you would have written that if you weren't somewhat sure of how I felt.

What was I thinking about when that photograph was taken? I thought you knew, Davey. I was thinking of you.

Sue

Chicago, Illinois, U.S.A.
August 20, 1915

My dear Sue,

Do you realize how nervous I've been, waiting for your reply? If I were a betting man, I would've put a large wager on you not replying at all. But the small part of me that saw signs and portents in every letter you sent, the part of me that not only read between the lines but above and below, that part would have put a wager on you writing back and knowing exactly what I was talking about. I'm glad that part of me won the bet, for the prize is so much greater.

What happens now? If you lived down the street in Chicago, I'd ask you to dinner. Or maybe not. What does one do with a married woman, apart from leave her alone?

See, I'm going to make a muddle of this. Whatever "this" is. You've seen how I've been failing at just about everything I've set my mind to these days. A guy with nothing going for him but guts. Why would you want a guy like me?

Wondering,
David

Isle of Skye
6 September 1915

Davey, Davey, Davey,

You're not a worrier. Why are you thinking so hard about this? The past three years, we've let things fall as they may, and love happened. Do we need to plan out what comes next? Do we even need to know?

I hope you realise that I've never thought of you as "a guy with nothing going for him but guts." If you only knew how you keep me going, how you keep me waking up, simply because I know you're thinking of me. You moved me to write again when I thought my muse had fled. You reminded me that I'm not just a lonely recluse. I have something more now. I have you.

Do you really think you need to prove yourself to me? Do you think you have to do anything but continue to be there? That's all I ask. Just be there.

> Thinking of you,
> Sue

Chicago, Illinois, U.S.A.
September 28, 1915

Sue,

So much has happened here. You'll never guess—I'm going over to the front! Harry saw an ad for the American Ambulance Field Service, looking for volunteers to drive ambulances for the French Army. Wilson can't get off his duff and let us Americans into the war, so we'll have to find our own way in.

Think of it! Driving an auto as fast as I can, shells whizzing by overhead, men's lives actually dependent on me driving as recklessly and as fearlessly as I can. Can you think of anything more perfect for me? I couldn't manage as a teacher, but this . . . this I can do.

We don't get paid, but I have a small trust fund set up by my grandfather. Harry has already said we'll pool our resources once we get to France and, if we have to eat canned beans or brown bread or whatnot every day, so be it. No money forth-coming from my father!

Harry and I went over there for dinner last night to break the news. My mother left the table, dabbing at her eyes, and my fa-ther asked, "Why on earth are you going to France?" Harry leaned back in his chair and said, "Hell if I know. But it will be a damned fine adventure," then saluted my father with his glass of Madeira. My father turned purple and I thought he would have an apoplexy.

We have a few things to do here. Have to get a typhoid inoc-ulation, which will take a couple of weeks, and we're waiting for official letters from the headquarters of the American Ambu-lance to send to the State Department. We'll need letters of credit from our banks. We have supplies to get together (boots, sweaters, driving gloves), but we'll get our uniforms in Paris. And photographs! I need a dozen or so copies of my passport photo for licenses and identification cards. So much to do and we're trying to get it done as quickly as we can.

We officially sign on for a six-month term of service and can reenlist for three months at a time after that. Both Harry and I told them to count us in for at least a year. We're not the kind of guys who do anything halfway.

I finally feel as if I've found my purpose in life, Sue, and I can hardly wait to get there!

    Exuberant,

    Davey

Isle of Skye
15 October 1915

You stupid, stupid boy! Did you expect me to be *happy* about
this plan of yours? With a husband at the front and a brother
crippled from this blasted war, what on earth did you think I'd
really say?

I don't even understand why you're doing this. What do you
owe France? Or any other nation, for that matter? Why do you
feel duty-bound to get involved in the foolishness on this side of
the ocean? What makes you think this war has anything to do
with you?

Did you stop to think for a moment about me in all this?
How, only recently, I offered my heart up to you, tentatively,
hesitantly, not trusting my own feelings but trusting you implic-
itly? And now you've trampled all over it in your haste to run
off.

All I wanted was for you to be there. Why are you leaving?

Chicago, Illinois, U.S.A.
October 31, 1915

Dear Sue,

I know you're angry; please don't be. Talk of "duty" and
"patriotism" aside, how could you really expect me to pass up
on this, the ultimate adventure?

My mother's been floating around the house, red-eyed and
sniffling. My father still isn't speaking to me. And yet I feel like

I'm doing something right. I messed up in college. I messed up at work. Hell, I even messed up with Lara. I was beginning to think there was no place in the world for a guy whose highest achievement included a sack full of squirrels. Nobody seemed to want my bravado and impulsivity before. You know this is right for me, Sue. You of all people, who seem to know things about me before I myself do. You know this is right.

I'm leaving tomorrow for New York and have to trust my mother to mail this letter. When you read it, I'll be on a ship somewhere in the Atlantic. Even though we get a reduction on our fares if we sail the French Line, Harry and I are bound for England. He has Minna over there waiting for him. And I . . . I have you. Like knights of old, neither of us can head off to fight without a token from our love to tuck into our sleeve.

I'll be landing in Southampton sometime in the middle of November and will be going up to London. Sue, say that you'll meet me this time. I know it's easy for me to ask, far easier than it is for you to leave your sanctuary there on Skye. Don't let me go off to the front without having touched you for the first time, without having heard your voice say my name. Don't let me go off to the front without a memory of you in my heart.

Yours . . . always and forever,
Davey

POST OFFICE TELEGRAPHS

S 8.25 SOUTHAMPTON

15 NOV 15

E. DUNN ISLE OF SKYE=

HEADING TO LONDON WILL BE AT THE LANGHAM AGAIN

    WILL WIRE WHEN WE ARRIVE=

        D+

POST OFFICE TELEGRAPHS

S 15.07 PORTREE

15 NOV 15

D GRAHAM THE LANGHAM HOTEL=

THURSDAY AT HALF PAST SIX KINGS CROSS STATION SPE-

    CIAL SCOTCH EXPRESS=

WAIT FOR ME MY LOVE=

        SUE+

Chapter Ten

~

Margaret

Edinburgh
Wednesday, 7 August 1940

Dear Uncle Finlay,

My mother is a contained person. I'm not sure what she was like before I was born, but as I know her, she keeps everything held tightly to her chest. She never talks about the past, apart from her childhood. Nothing about friendship, nothing about yearning, nothing about love or loss. She simply moves through the present.

She has her routines, the things she does every day. In the morning, she walks. Along the Water of Leith. Around Holyrood Park. Along the beaches and docks, before they were fortified. To the farthest edges of the city and then back again. No matter the weather, no matter the season, she's out walking. She'll bring back a sprig of gorse just to put it on her pillow and

smell it; she'll bring back the first snowdrop of winter to remember the promise of spring.

When she's finished walking, she goes to St. Mary's Cathedral and sits. Not for the Mass; she goes when the church is
quiet, empty, still. The priests, they all know her by name. She's
the one who comes only to sit and bask in the peace of the cathedral.

But this war here suddenly unsettled my mother beyond
what I've ever seen before. Before disappearing, she started to
carry her brown Bible in her handbag. She didn't walk as far or
as long. She began to crumble.

I know that war is frightening, especially when you've already lived through one. But why Mother? Why now?

    Margaret Dunn

Glasgow
8 August

Margaret,

    Maybe the better question is, "Why not everyone else?"
Why doesn't everyone over the age of twenty-five freeze up at
the very mention of war?

Elspeth was never one caught up in the past. Even as a lass,
her face was always turned towards the sun. But she never could
keep hold of her feelings. Our brother Alasdair always said she
wanted too badly for everyone to love her. Back then, we did.

That was Elspeth's problem. She cared too much. When the
war started to threaten everyone around her, she reached out

and grabbed for whatever she could hold on to, trying to catch any bit of happiness she could. As if life really works that way. She set herself up to be shattered, and she was. None of us could stop the choices she made. It's little surprise to me that this war reminds her of the other. Of the time when she broke our family in pieces.

Finlay Macdonald

Edinburgh
Friday, 9 August 1940

Dear Uncle Finlay,

Is that it? Is that why Mother has never spoken of her life on Skye beyond girlhood? Why she's never mentioned that I have an uncle staying just a short train ride away in Glasgow? What did my churchgoing, nature-loving mother do to break a family to pieces?

Was it because of Sue?

Margaret

Glasgow
10 August

Margaret,

You should be asking her these questions. I cannot help you. I don't know anyone named Sue.

Finlay Macdonald

Edinburgh
Monday, 12 August 1940

Dear Uncle Finlay,

I can't ask her. She's gone. She left.

Last month, a bomb fell on our street. We didn't have much damage apart from broken windows, but, in the wreck, I found letters I'd never seen before. Piles and piles of letters. The one I picked up was addressed to "Sue" from an American called Davey. I don't know who they are or what was in the rest, because, the next morning, both my mother and the letters were gone.

So I can't ask her. I can't even find her. If I weren't desperate, why would I be looking up mysterious uncles?

Margaret

Glasgow
13 August

The American? That is what this is about? After all these years, still the American?

I couldn't stop the choices she made then and I certainly can't now. Please don't write to me again.

Finlay Macdonald

Edinburgh
Wednesday, 14 August 1940

Dear Paul,

It was working. Uncle Finlay was telling me about my
mother in dribs and drabs. There was something that he said
"broke our family in pieces." And then I mentioned the letter
and the American and he's stopped writing. I don't know what I
said! How does this American fit into my mother's story? What
happened all those years ago?

Margaret

London
10 August 1940

My Margaret,

I must have written dozens of letters explaining to you where
I went. But then I looked through the letters I'd brought with
me and wondered if you'd even still be in Edinburgh. Maybe
you've already set off in search of secrets.

One of my letters is missing: the letter you picked up off the
floor that night. I know exactly which one it is. A letter where a
silly, wonderful boy joins a war to prove himself a man. Where
he begs the woman he loves to set off into the Great Unknown.
London, his arms—both equally intimidating. Where he dares
her to trust him. Ridiculous that such a boy could have not a
fear in the world, while the woman waiting at the other end of

the letters is terrified of going beyond the water's edge. Terrified of meeting the wielder of that pen. Terrified to open up her heart again.

And so, when the war tore through my walls and let memories come tumbling out, where to go but London? I had to see if ghosts still drifted here the way they always drift around Edinburgh.

Once, too long ago, I fell in love. Unexpected, heady love. I didn't want to let it go. His name was David, and his soul bloomed with beauty. He called me "Sue" and wrote me letters, emotion pinned to the page with each stroke of the pencil. When he wrote, I didn't feel so alone up on my little island.

But the war seethed then, and it wasn't the time or place for new love. In a war, emotions can be confused, people can disappear, minds can change. Perhaps I was wrong to fall in love so suddenly. What happened all those years ago, what happened with David: It cost me my brother. It cost me a lot.

If I could do it differently, would I? Make different choices that would keep my family together? Make different choices that would keep me from spending the rest of my life alone?

I've spent the past twenty years wondering that. But on the train to London, surrounded by Davey's letters, I realised that I wouldn't have done a thing differently. Of course, I wish that Finlay never left. But those few bright years of beauty, despite the rest of fumbling loneliness, I wouldn't have traded for the world. All of the choices I made then brought me you. And that makes everything that came before worth it.

I hope you forgive me for not telling you everything. But the

past is past. I love the present, with you. I never wanted anything to rattle that.

Happy birthday, my Margaret. When I find the answers I
need, I'll come home to you.

Love,
Mother

Chapter Eleven

~

Elspeth

The Langham, London
27 November 1915

Davey,

You've only just left, are probably now settling down in your seat, listening to the train rumble out of London. I'm sorry I didn't see you to the station. Truly I am. I had no faith in myself. I knew if I had gone to the station with you, I would've clung on to your arm and not let go. Now, though, I do regret not going, not getting one more chance to see your dear face.

I have to admit that, once the tears dried, I was quite angry with you. I suppose I thought I could somehow convince you to stay. If I gave it all to you, you wouldn't be able to leave. Not that I would've given you any less of myself. How could I? Everything about these past nine days was perfect.

On the train down, though, I was terrified, more terrified

than I'd been to climb onto that ferry, and that I had to walk onto with eyes closed and breath held. With every pitch of the boat, I wished myself back at home, where the ground didn't move. But the train was even worse. It wasn't only taking me away from home, into the unknown. It was taking me towards you.

I know you're in love with me. Never doubt that, my boy. Three years of deliberate word choices, neat turns of phrase, the "Sue" on the envelope written with extra care. I know I had no reason to worry about our meeting. Yet I did. All that, you did for a pen-and-paper Elspeth, a witty and worldly woman who offhandedly sends letters to Americans, who argues about books and writes poetry at the drop of a hat.

But those poems I write by dim candlelight, as birds roost in the thatch above. I wipe stinging eyes to read your letters, crouched by the smoky swirl of the peat fire. None of my neighbours thinks of me beyond That Odd Bird, Elspeth, the one who walks into town with a book in hand rather than a spindle. As the train chugged closer to London, I couldn't help but wonder whether you'd think the same.

But then I stepped into King's Cross Station, met your eyes across the crowd, and all my fears melted. You saw past the elegant pink dress, past the hair I'd spent the past hour straightening, past my attempts to look like the kind of woman who travels across the country to meet fascinating Americans. You saw the real Elspeth. You saw me.

Did you really think I wouldn't recognize you without that silly red carnation in your lapel? Did you think I wouldn't see you for the romantic I know you to be? I've pulled out and stared at your picture enough that I think it may be burned onto the inside of my eyelids. Now I know my dreams are the stuff of more than imagination.

But to see you in the flesh, in colour, is more than I could ever hope for. Did you know your eyes are the exact brown-green of the Scottish hills in wintertime? And you are so much taller than I would've guessed from your photos. You lost that mustache you'd taken such pains to grow, and your hair is shorter yet still invites fingers through all those sandy curls.

You seemed so shy when you met me at the station, almost as if you didn't know me at all. And I couldn't believe that my Davey, the boy who can blether on for pages about books and tree wars and his niece, couldn't think of more than ten words over supper! I think I prattled on enough for the both of us. I was nervous, though, dining at my very first restaurant. So many people, so many forks, and not an oatcake in sight. But when we walked back to the Langham, when you stopped my words with a kiss that left me breathless, that's when I saw the Davey I love. That's when I saw the fearless boy who stole my heart.

Ah, the Langham! I felt like a princess just walking through the front door. All marble and glass and electric lights, like a palace. Did you not expect me to come back to your room? It certainly seemed so, the way your eyes grew huge and your hands trembly when I suggested it. You dropped the key to the room five times; I counted. And there was nothing to be nervous about in the end.

I wish we could've stayed up there the whole time. Nine perfect days. Waking up and seeing that funny startled look in your eyes each morning to find me still there. Falling asleep in your arms with our drowsy conversation in the dark. I collected each word like a bead, to string together on my lonely nights back on Skye. Yours is the very first American accent I've ever heard. I like it best when it's saying, "I love you."

I know you had to leave. Even after all that, even after *me,* you had to leave. And I hate myself for hating it. I hate myself for wasting a single second of our precious time wishing things could be different.

Of course, I couldn't tell you any of this in person. I couldn't say much at all. The very sound of our voices was so . . . *odd.* So banal. I confess I couldn't wait to get back to my notepaper and pen to tell you how I felt. And to tell you how my mind is collaborating with my heart and my body to make me miss you unbelievably, more than I thought I could.

I love you. Stay safe. Stay safe for me.

Sue

The Langham, London
29 November 1915

My own boy,

You probably don't yet have my earlier letter, but I thought it could never be too soon to tell you again how much I miss you. The hotel seems so big and lonely without you (does the room echo or it just my imagination?). The scent of oranges linger in the air and I swear I can still see the shape of you in the mattress. As lovely as the Langham is, I shan't be too sad to leave. It isn't as lovely when you aren't here.

I went out shopping today. Davey, why didn't you tell me about all of the books? While out walking, I turned a corner and was confronted with a street packed full of bookshops. You may laugh, but even if I were to have let my imagination run loose, I never would've conjured up an image of an entire store filled with *nothing but books*. I'm afraid I looked quite the "country yokel," standing in the doorway of the first establishment I entered, staring around me goggle-eyed at the shelves upon shelves. It was Foyles, so of course it was some time before I re-emerged, blinking, into the sunlight. I swear I became lost a dozen times. The rest of the day I traipsed from one end of Charing Cross Road to the other, ducking into every single bookshop I passed, and not leaving without buying at least one thing. I became quite adept at saying, in an offhand sort of way, "Send this to the Langham," and then was flabbergasted at the stacks of parcels awaiting me at the hotel that evening.

I puzzled over what to get for you, Davey, my dear, as I know that you have only a limited amount of room in your kit bag. All a person really needs to get them through the vagaries of life are the Bible and W. S. (both of them). I guessed you already had a Bible, so I'm sending you Scott's *Lady of the Lake* and the most compact edition of Shakespeare's works I could find. And a little sliver of room left in the package which I've filled with Dryden. After all, "words are but pictures of our thoughts."

The funniest thing—I was greeted in one bookstore by a display of my own books. I must've looked amused as I picked up a copy of *Waves to Peinchorran*, as a salesclerk hurried up to me. "Twee little verse," she said, quite seriously. "The author lives up in the Highlands of Scotland. You get a lovely sense of their superstitions and almost primitive lifestyle." I nodded sagely, then took the book to the counter and signed the flyleaf with a very distinct "Elspeth Dunn." I handed the book back to the astonished salesclerk and said, with what I hope was an airy tone, "We're regular savages but don't *always* eat our own young."

I am running water for one more long, luxurious bath; a bath where I don't have to draw and heat the water myself. Just to sink back in the steamy water and rose oil is heaven itself. In the morning I'm meeting my publisher in Cecil Court (where he's promised me even more bookshops!), and then I'm heading back to the station to catch my train north. I'll write to you again when I get there, but I'll be crossing my fingers, my toes, and maybe even my eyes (when no one is looking) that there will be a letter from you waiting for me.

> With every inch of my being,
> Sue

Paris, France
December 5, 1915

My Sue,

What a surprise to get here and find not one but two letters from you waiting!

I've been busy, running from one end of Paris to the other, it seems, securing the necessary paperwork, buying my uniform and the last bits of equipment, taking my driving exam. Did I tell you that, when I was on the boat trip across the Atlantic, I had the childish urge to go to Paris first and then to London, so that I could greet you all kitted out in my uniform? I think I look quite well turned out. All dressed up, but nowhere to go!

Until we get to the front, we've been trying to enjoy what bit of time we have before we're really put to work. Our uniforms get us all sorts of boons—half-priced theater tickets, discounted drinks. It's been fun, but . . . it still doesn't seem like the "Gay Paree" I remember. Many of the theaters and music halls are shut or operate on shortened hours. Cafés are closed early, lights are dimmed on the street at night. Even so far from the trenches, it's a city at war.

The books are much appreciated, as I'm sure you knew the moment you bought them. You're determined to turn me into a poetry reader, aren't you? Haven't I told you that Elspeth Dunn is the only poet for me? I just have room left in my duffel bag for the Shakespeare, but Harry's going to read the Dryden and W. S. and then we'll swap.

My Bible is one that I've had since my First Communion. It's a slim little volume bound in limp brown leather with pages as thin as dragonfly wings, so it's the perfect size for my bag. My name is scrawled in the frontispiece in round, childish letters, and I have a lock of Evie's hair tucked somewhere in the Book of Ruth, so it can't help but remind me of home.

I also brought along my battered copy of *Huck Finn*, more for comfort than for reading, as I could probably recite the whole book verbatim. But that dog-eared book has been the first

thing in my suitcase when packing for anything stressful or
upheaving—hospital visits (of which, as you know, there have
been more than a few), first ocean voyage, going away to college, moving to the apartment. I take it out, read it straightaway,
and it immediately makes me feel that I'm back curled in the
green armchair in my parents' library. It only stands to reason
that I'd bring it along here.

Perhaps it's superstitious, but I also view the book somewhat
as a lucky charm. My mother bought it to read aloud to Evie
and me when we had the measles. We finished reading the book
and then, the next day, Evie's fever broke. I've always somehow
associated that collective sigh of relief with *Huck Finn*.

You may rightly wonder, why does the invincible Mort need
a lucky charm? Well, Sue, I'm afraid. For the first time in my
life I'm really afraid of something tangible. I was fine on the
boat ride over, even eager for what awaited me in France. What
I overlooked, though, was what I would find in London. I found
something worth coming back for. I found you, Sue.

The boy who never shied away from any form of daredev-
ilry, brought to his knees by a woman he only just met. But what
a woman she is! When you stepped off the train and that shaft of
sunlight found its way through the glass in the roof to set you
aglow, even an atheist would've seen the finger of God in that.

Even after you stepped into the shadows, you glowed like a
candle the rest of the day. You spoke, and I heard a chorus of
seraphim. You laid your hand on my arm when we were leaving, but I felt the touch of wings. A bit flowery, I'll give you, but
such was my state of mind. I laid eyes on you, there was that
shaft of sunlight, and I was suddenly terrified. Terrified you

would disappear in a cloud of bubbles, terrified I might be hit by a bus in the next instant, terrified the world would end before our world had even begun.

Not until we were in the taxicab and you tumbled nearly onto my lap as we edged that corner was I truly aware you were flesh and blood. My skin memorized every place you touched, and that feeling didn't diminish for the rest of the afternoon. I don't know if that one little incident made as much of an impression on you as it did me, but it reminded me whom I was with. Not an unreachable angel but a woman I know better than I know the lines in my own palm.

I was still terrified, though. I didn't want to make a wrong move. That first evening was perfect. Dinner, dancing, strolling through Regent's Park. I didn't want to ruin it by suggesting anything improper. I wanted to—oh, God, did I want to!—but I could never have brought myself to ask.

I have a small confession to make. Or maybe you've guessed it already. That was the first time I was with a woman. With a woman in *that* way, I mean. Remember when you pulled the sheet over my shoulders? I wasn't shivering because of the cold; I was scared to death. Of course I had an *idea* of what to do—all guys talk about that—but no concrete list of instructions. I didn't want to go about it the wrong way. And then you laughed and you kissed me again, and I realized in that laugh that you were every bit as nervous as I was. How was I to know that there really *was* no list of instructions? How was I to know that that could be . . . that?

You're right, though, it was a shame we had to leave that room at all during those blessed nine days, but I suppose it had to be done. I wouldn't have missed being best man, and I think Minna was happy to have another woman as witness aside from her mother. Harry had to peel Minna off him at the station. She tossed her hair and blew him a saucy kiss as he climbed on board. I happened to glance back and see her resolve crumble, and, for an instant, she looked like a little girl. With all of her carrying on, I sometimes forget how young she really is.

As we sat in the register building, waiting with Minna and Harry, I couldn't help but think of our future, Sue. When I come back from the front, when I've served my year, what do we do then? What options do we have?

Harry is grumbling at me to turn off the light and go to bed. Now he's just thrown a boot at me, the cantankerous bastard. We have just a few more hours before we have to be up, so perhaps I will oblige him, as long as he doesn't use me as a target any longer.

You know, writing this all to you has helped calm my fears somewhat. As long as I still have your letters, a lifeline running to me all the way from Scotland, I will be okay. I told you I brought the book along with me as a lucky charm, but you, Sue, you are my lucky charm.

Loving you,
David

Edinburgh
12 December 1915

My love,

Your letter preceded me to Edinburgh, and it was a very be-
wildered Chrissie who greeted me at the door to her flat. I had
taken my time working my way back up to Scotland, spending a
few days in York and a few days touring the abbeys in the Scottish Borders. Off my island, I resolved to see as much as I could.
I thought it would be a bit of a lark to appear on Chrissie's
doorstep. To say she was shocked to see me would be an under-
statement.

It's quite overwhelming to go from living by myself in an
isolated cottage to living on a busy block in a wee flat full of
children and noise. At least Chrissie has given me a room of my
own, putting me up on the sofa in the little sitting room. I am
quite dizzy most of the time and seem to have had a constant
headache from their chatter, but it's been lovely. Chrissie and
Alasdair's children have grown so! I suppose it has probably
been six or seven years since they moved from Skye, so it's not
at all surprising. I wouldn't have expected them to shrink. My
niece, Emily, is turning eleven now and is quite the lady. The
boys, Allie and Robbie, are eight and six and are quite a handful.
When I last saw Robbie, he wasn't even walking yet, and here
he is, running and telling jokes and doing sums in his head. All
of them are so full of life that it seems almost indecent in this
time of war.

Incidentally, you *will* tell me if there is anything you need,
Davey? Prices may be sky-high here in Edinburgh, but I imag-

ine they are still lower than what you are finding in France.
I bought enough books in London that I can certainly spare
some to send on, once you've found room in your kit bag. Toss
away a mug or a few bits of weaponry. Make room for the really
important things, dear!

I know exactly what you mean about your much-loved copy
of *Huck Finn* being a source of comfort and even of luck. Because I rarely leave my cottage, I don't think I have as many of
those anxious moments as you do, but I most definitely did when
I bribed Willie to blindfold me and toss me on the bottom of
that ferry. My lucky charm is a piece of amber, the clear colour
of honey. Finlay brought it back for me the first time he sailed
off with Da. That stone led to my fascination with geology. I
carried it in my pocket for the longest time and, when I was feeling blue, would take it out to examine, hoping to discover the
magic it held. When reading aloud in school or sitting for
exams, I would feel for its reassuring shape in my pocket. The
amber is worn quite smooth now and has an appealing little
groove where my thumb fits. It only stands to reason that it
would be the first thing in my suitcase when I left Skye.

It's funny to hear you go on about that shaft of sunlight
falling as I stepped off the train. I know just what you were
talking about, but I'm afraid I didn't view it quite as poetically
as you did. I was trying to scan the station to find you when
that ridiculous sunlight broke right through the window and
shone into my eyes. And that accidental tumble in the taxicab?
Perhaps I would've felt the same current of electricity if I hadn't
been so utterly embarrassed at landing in an undignified heap on
your lap.

Not to make light of your romantic impressions, my darling. I *am* a poet, after all, and capable of being every bit as sentimental.

I was certainly nervous to meet you but, truly, I didn't dream you'd be nervous as well. And terrified? I didn't think you had ever heard of the word. I might have ventured to say that you'd done this before—declared your undying adoration to a woman you'd never laid eyes on, joined the French Army for an excuse to cross the Atlantic, and then lured her to an extravagant London hotel.

I did see a slight slip in your confidence when we got up to your room. I didn't know for sure that it was your first time, but I wondered. You are right, though: I was scared too. I think all of the experience in the world couldn't prepare someone for the very first time they are with a person they love. Was there really anything to be worried about? It obviously all worked out quite well—or we wouldn't have repeated it so many times!

I don't know what options are open to us in the future. But do we need to worry about it now? The world has enough worry without adding another skein to the tangle. You just concentrate on staying out of the way of the shells and bullets, and I'll concentrate on writing to you and loving you more every day that passes.

Yours,

Sue

Chapter Twelve

～

Margaret

Edinburgh
Wednesday, 14 August 1940

Dear Uncle Finlay,

I know you've asked me not to write again, but I'm old enough to not always do what I'm asked.

My mother wrote. She's in London. If you'd told me that a month ago, I wouldn't have believed it. In my lifetime, she's never been out of Edinburgh. But since learning about her life on Skye, I'm ready to believe anything.

She told me about David, "the American," that she'd been in love with him for years. She hadn't expected it, yet she couldn't do without it. And, seeing her face as she gathered up those letters from the floor, I think she still can't. But, you may be happy to know, she did. She has. Apart from me, my mother has been alone for the past two decades. Until I saw her the night the bomb fell, the night the war tore through her heart, I never would've known. I never would've seen in that instant how lonely she was. I never would've learned what she'd lost.

She's never talked about being loved or being left behind. She's never talked about my father. What happened to David? All of those years ago, what happened to them?

Margaret

Edinburgh
Wednesday, 14 August 1940

Dear Paul,

If you can believe it, my mother is in London. Chasing after memories. And I'm here, trying to ask the right questions of my disagreeable uncle, chasing after the same.

She wrote to me, finally, and offered something in the way of explanation. Paul, my mother was "Sue." Those letters, they were all for her. Some grand romance, in the middle of the last war. With an American! I don't know how my mother ever met an American up on the Isle of Skye. And, whatever happened with him, it led to her brother leaving.

As I picked up pen to write her back and ask all the questions still swirling around in my head, I realized she gave no address. Only "London." I could send a letter to every hotel in London and never find her. I can't help but think that, if I discover where she has been, it will lead me to where she is now.

Paul, am I doing wrong to be digging into her life? Should I just leave the past alone, the way she wants? The way my uncle wants? The way everyone seems to want me to do?

Margaret

16 August 1940

Dear Maisie,

All of these night sorties make me realise how the past doesn't help when we're put in a tight spot. Memories are all well and good to hold on to, but it's the promise of making new memories that helps me to push through.

I never told you, but I was shot down over France, right before the evacuations. I knew if I admitted it to you in Plymouth, you'd be so worried, you'd never let me get back on that train. It wasn't bad—I jumped before I hit the ground—and, as you saw, I wasn't worse for wear. I joined in with everyone fleeing for the beaches at Dunkirk. And there I saw none of our planes. Just the damned Luftwaffe, trying to keep our lads from making it onto the ships.

Despite what everyone said, we were over there in France—the R.A.F.—just not at the beaches. We were inland, trying to keep the Jerrys from ever getting as far as the coast. But all the men waiting to be evacuated, all the men being strafed on the sand, they didn't know that. I waited there on that beach with them, in my uniform, trying to ignore the glares and the grumblings of "Where's the R.A.F.?"

If I stopped to remember how it feels to duck down in a strafing, with nothing between me and the bullets but my helmet and laced hands over my neck, if I stopped to remember the miles of slogging, only to see the lads in front of me stumble upon a mine, if I stopped to remember crouching in the dark, not knowing whether the whine of the next shell had my name on it, if I stopped to remember the muttered comments around me of lads who didn't know that I'd been up there, doing my job, I'd never move forward. I have to just keep telling myself that I'll be back with you in no time. Nothing else I can do.

But, as much as I try to push the past aside so that I keep moving forward, nothing is holding you back that way. You have more questions than memories, more mystery than enlightenment. You have to look behind you. The present and the future are built on the past. I know that you want to find where you came from before you'll know where to go.

My lass, don't give up. Disagreeable uncles? They are no match for you.

> Love,
> Paul

Edinburgh
Monday, 19 August 1940

Dear Uncle Finlay,

She mentioned you in the letter she sent from London.

She told me how she was so happy with David, so deliriously

in love, but that it had cost her her brother. That you'd left Skye and she wished you never did.

She didn't explain the reasons why, and I won't ask. Of course I'm curious—who wouldn't be about a family schism spoken about only in whispers?—but I know it's not my business. You didn't approve of Americans? Wartime romance? I only hope the reason was big enough, threatening enough, lasting enough, to make decades away from your family worthwhile.

But know this: Whether or not she regrets the choices she made, she does regret losing you. If she'd known in the past twenty years where you were, she would have told you that herself. She'd already lost one brother; what made you think she could bear to lose another?

Margaret

Glasgow
20 August

Margaret,

She's telling you the truth. She was in love with the American. More than that—she made it sound like a fairy tale. A chance letter that sparked years of correspondence, finding blots of love between each word on the page. Depending on the post more than the tides and the moon. Even war couldn't stop what blossomed between them.

She didn't lie about either the American or how she felt. But it wasn't the time for all that. It wasn't the time to fall in love.

When Elspeth began writing to the American, she was already married.

Finlay Macdonald

Edinburgh
Wednesday, 21 August 1940

Dear Uncle Finlay,

There are so many women around here with a "Mrs." before their name but no man at home. A black-edged photograph on the mantel of a man in uniform hints at a story better forgotten. Because my mother has always refused to answer my questions, I've assumed her story was the same—some sad youthful marriage that ended on a battlefield somewhere. Lately I'd started to wonder if it could've been David. But now . . . She was already married?

Who is my father? Please, Uncle Finlay, I have to know! What is my story?

Margaret

London, England
6 August 1940

Dear Sir or Madam,

Many years ago, a family named Graham lived at this address. I do not know if they still stay there or if they have moved from Chicago, but I would appreciate any information you could supply. I have been out of touch with the family and would like to find them.

If you have any information about their whereabouts or, indeed, if you are a member of the Graham family, can you please contact me? You can write to me at the Langham Hotel, London. I thank you in advance.

Sincerely,

Mrs. Elspeth Dunn

Chapter Thirteen

~

Elspeth

Paris, France
December 17, 1915

My Sue,

It looks more and more like we'll be spending Christmas beneath the Eiffel Tower. It goes without saying that I would rather be spending Christmas in Edinburgh, on Skye, or wherever you are. Harry is all fine and good as a companion but not exactly the person I hope to catch unawares beneath the mistletoe.

We're living in the dormitory above the hospital with the other American volunteers. After the first few days of trying to muddle our way through brisk French, it was so comforting to hear a good ol' American twang. We sleep in one huge room with beds lining all of the sides. Only one shower for all of us guys, and a cold one at that. No lights at night, save for a single

lamp in the center of the room, so I'm working on this letter in
snatched moments during the day. It's not much, but, at least for
now, it's home!

I think both Harry and I had this vision of driving the ambulances directly off the boat and into the front line of danger.
Even though we've not been sent to the front, we haven't been
idle. I've been assigned a little ambulance with another chap,
name of McGee. When the hospital trains come in from the
front, we have to zip to the freight yards at the end of Rue de la
Chapelle to collect their ragged passengers. Some are quite serious, but they are the ones deemed fit enough to make the train
journey. I suppose the worst cases don't even make it onto the
train. We load them up and then hurtle through the dark streets
to the makeshift hospitals scattered around the city. I like to pretend the Grim Reaper drives next to me, racing me to the hospital to see who gets the men in the back of my ambulance. My
little truck is light and fast and so the Grim Reaper always ends
up a street behind me, with a mouthful of dust.

The work here really is pretty light, though. Trains seem to
mostly come at night. We have to spend some time in the garage
keeping our vehicles in tune. Still, we have plenty of opportunity to explore Paris during the day. Harry and I sightsee like
tourists, catch flicks half-price at the Gaumont Palace. We've
been combing the French bookshops with as much joy as you
did their London counterparts. Parked at our favorite café, we
slog through Dumas and Boussenard (untranslated) in an attempt to dust off our much-disused high school French.

Not quite Christmas, but I'll include your gifts. I wish I
could be there to give them to you in person. Will you do some-

thing for me? As Christmas Eve turns into Christmas Day, right at the stroke of midnight, step outside and tilt your face up at the moon. Taste the snowflakes on your lips and imagine they are my lips touching yours. I will step outside at exactly the same time. I promise. No matter if I'm still in Paris or somewhere else in France, I'll close my eyes and I'll imagine the same. Perhaps it could really come true, if even just for an instant. If a miracle such as our Lord's birth could occur on a night like this, then it is no great feat for our spirits to meet.

    Love,

    Davey

Edinburgh

Late Christmas Eve, wee sma' 'oors of Christmas Day, 1915

My love,

    It's late on Christmas Eve, the children are "nestled all snug in their beds," and I'm the only one still awake to wait for St. Nicholas.

    Chrissie and I sat up late, drinking far too many mugs of mulled wine. It was the first time we've really been able to sit and catch up on the past six or so years with no children running circles around us. Not much to tell. Apart from the husband-running-away-while-dashing-American-seduces, the past six years have been nothing more than crofting and writing. Your name slipped out, just once, but something on my face must've made her kiss my forehead instead of asking another question, and she went off to bed.

I poured out another mug of wine and watched her through the open doorway, climbing into the bed she's kept empty since Alasdair's death, and knew she wouldn't understand even if I were to tell her about you. Alone, she'll stay married to Alasdair the rest of her life. And so I retired to the sitting room with my candle, notebook, wine, and secrets.

I've opened the window, swung my legs out on the window-sill to open up your present. Ah . . . a bottle of real French per-fume! An appropriate gift for a lovesick boy to send from Paris. And, oh, Davey, the necklace is simply lovely! A pearl so per-fect, like a single drop of moonlight. Thank you.

The mantel clock—two minutes fast—is chiming out mid-night, so I'm leaning out the window. Did you feel that, my love? Not a snowflake against your cheek; my lips tasting you. Not a whisper of wind in your ear; my voice whispering, "I love you." Did you smell that hint of Ambre Antique on the air? I was there.

I know the children will be up early, stampeding into the kitchen to see if St. Nicholas has come, so I should go to bed, al-though I'd sooner stay up with you and this letter. We may be far apart but, at least for a moment tonight, we tried to erase that distance.

Merry, merry Christmas, my Davey.

Elspeth

Paris, France
January 1, 1916

Dearest Sue,

I was getting quite impatient for your letter! I suppose I
didn't think about the holidays delaying the mail. That knowledge didn't lessen my impatience, but at least I knew it was late
because you waited until Christmas to write and not because
you'd found yourself another brash American cowboy.

The wristwatch is perfect! You remembered I've been wanting one to replace my pocket watch. This will be much handier
over here. I keep my pocket watch buttoned inside my jacket,
and it's not so easy to pull out when I need to check the time
(quite frequently these days).

Your letter and gift provided a speck of light in what was
otherwise a black and thundery week. The weather wasn't quite
so dire; I'm afraid it was my mood that was black and thundery.
I was down enough about spending Christmas away from my
family (yes, I even missed my mother's fruitcake!), but then
Harry got his orders.

Throughout all this, Harry and I have been inseparable, and
then they had to go and send him off into the teeth of the battle,
leaving me behind with sniveling McGee. All because Harry
happened to be ahead of me in line as we were signing up. Without my family, without even you, Sue, I figured at least to have
Harry to spend Christmas with. Instead, I was faced with the
choice of hanging out with Johnson and the rest of the degener-
ates down in the red-light district or sitting in the dormitory listening to McGee read aloud from old letters from his mother.

I ended up crawling into bed with Dryden (becoming quite dog-eared now) until lights-out.

Even though Harry had nothing to do with the decision, I was quite cross with him while he was packing up. I grumbled and called him names, many gleaned from the copy of Shakespeare sitting on my bed. I particularly liked "monstrous malefactor" and "unlick'd bear whelp." He just laughed at me, punched me in the shoulder in the male version of the tender embrace, and tossed a spare pair of his socks on my bed.

It's a running joke between the two of us. Right around the time we first met, Harry and I had gotten ourselves into some sort of mischief on our way home from school. I don't remember exactly what it was but something that left him without his hat and me without my boots or socks. We got to Harry's house first, and I begged him to lend me something to wear, as I knew the direst punishments imaginable awaited the boy who walked in the front door barefoot on Mother's "at home" day. Harry was reluctant—our friendship was still very new, mind you—but finally relented, after making me cross my eyes and spit over my shoulder to swear I'd return the boots and socks. He told me later he didn't think he'd ever see either again. I rather liked Harry, though, and hoped to become better friends, so I brought back the socks the very next day.

After that, it became a thing between us. A pair of socks was a promise to see each other again. I set off for college with his fine white dress socks folded in my suitcase, and he embarked across the Atlantic with a pair of my sturdy wools in his steamer. So I suppose that, since I have his socks, I'll *have* to see him again. Even if he is an unlick'd bear whelp.

I was able to sneak outside at midnight on Christmas Eve, as
promised. I closed my eyes and stood as still as I could, trying to
remember just how your fingers pressed on my shoulders, how
your hair tickled my chin, how your body measured the length
of mine. I caught the faint smell of flowers and had the wild
thought that perhaps it worked, that, for a brief moment, our
spirits had somehow transcended the distance between us.

But it was soon replaced by a whiff of cigarettes and raucous
laughter. Johnson, Pate, and Diggens stumbled into the quadrangle, a *cocotte* on each arm. The girls wore skirts nearly up
to their knees and filled the courtyard with the reek of cheap
cologne. Pate already had a hand under one of those short skirts.
"Attendre un moment, m'petites," slurred Diggens in ghastly
French, before disappearing into the dormitory. Whether for
his "French letters" or for a piss, I couldn't tell. Maybe both.
Need I say that my moment was ruined?

Johnson spotted me and demanded to know why my "pansy
ass" was lurking around outside by myself rather than going
after tail with them. I ignored him (with enormous self-
restraint!) and tried to move farther down the quadrangle, but
he followed, taunting. For whatever reason, he seems to find it
unnatural that I won't come out to the brothels. I don't know
what it is about me that infuriates him so much, as I don't see
him pestering McGee, and McGee is perhaps the archetypal
"pansy ass."

Johnson was drunk and determined to pick a fight, throwing
all sorts of insults, many revolving around my questionable gender and my alleged choices of barnyard lovers. For my part, I
couldn't think of a response aside from "unlick'd bear whelp"

and "mad mustachio purple-hued maltworm," neither of which I think Bill S. intended for such a situation. Then he tossed a verbal grenade (one I shan't repeat) that hit a bit too close to home, and I started for him. I think I would've gotten into a fight if the door to the ward hadn't opened. I saw the night nurse silhouetted in the rectangle of light and I melted back into the building, hurrying up to the dormitory. When I looked out the window, Johnson, Pate, and the girls had disappeared and a very confused Diggens stood in the yard being scolded by the nurse.

Believe me, Sue, neither fighting nor being alone is how I'd hoped to spend my Christmas this year. The only thing that made it all bearable was the chance that, for at least an instant at the stroke of midnight, we touched hands across the miles.

Well, Sue, the *mère* who owns the café is wiping down mugs and giving me a pointed look. A quick glance at my new wristwatch shows that I've been here for much longer than I thought. I will close for now, but I will be watching the post every day for your next letter.

    Love you,
    Davey

Edinburgh
7 January 1916

Davey,

What was it that Johnson said that "hit a bit too close to home"? You can't tell a thrilling story like that and then leave out the "punch line," as you Americans would say.

I've just received a letter from my mother. She's finally letting Willie enlist. He's been wearing her down over the past year and a half. Finlay won't be going back to the front, so she is secure in at least one son surviving the war.

Who knows what she thought when I disappeared? I didn't tell anyone I was leaving—aside from Willie, that is, and he didn't know why. We snuck from the cottage while Da was checking the lobster traps and Màthair was down on the shingle gathering up seaweed for the garden. I left a wee note saying there was something I had to do and I would write but it would be at least a fortnight before I returned. I knew it would be some time before they could decipher my scrawl (how *do* you do it, Davey?). I was fairly confident that neither would think to check the pier for me and that I could be halfway to London before anyone got the idea to question the ferryman. Willie loves a good adventure, and I was certain he wouldn't give it away too soon, no matter how fit to bursting he was. I'm going straight home from Edinburgh and have the whole train trip home to concoct a convincing story as to what gave me enough courage to cross the water by myself. Any suggestions?

So Willie is enlisting and he is coming through Edinburgh. He was supposed to arrive this morning, but the train must have been delayed. I'll have a few days to show him around the city before he officially enters the army and ceases to have any fun. Although you seem to paint a different picture, picking fights, going about with French whores . . . Perhaps war is more delightful than I thought!

Are you having fun, my Davey? All of the seriousness and the grim aspect of this aside, are you finding things to make you happy? You sound content in your letters. Lazy days reading in Parisian cafés, peppered with those bursts of excitement and adventure you love so well, driving pell-mell down the streets and alleys. A woman writing you passionate letters from Scotland . . .

Which books should I send next? Let's see, I'll look through the collection that I've amassed thus far in my travels. . . . I have a slim volume of Yeats (what "pilgrim soul" can resist Yeats?), a book of George Darley's poetry; what else do I have that you might enjoy? Aha! Perfect: *The Letters of Abélard and Héloïse.* Though promise me that our affair won't end as tragically. I couldn't bear a convent.

Edinburgh has been lovely, but I'm getting wistful for my fair isle. I miss the peat smoke, the tang of the bog myrtle, the warm smell of hay in the byre.

Willie's just arrived. I'll end now and post this while we're out. I love you.

E

Paris, France
January 12, 1916

Dear Sue,

At last, at last, to the front! A guy named Quinn and I have
been called up. We haven't yet been told where exactly we're
going, but we've been assigned to the famous Section One.
I don't know if it's the same ambulance section Harry is in,
but I have a pair of socks to return to him just in case.

No, Sue, please don't ask what it is that Johnson said. Not
only did he use language not fit for the ears of a pirate, but the
gist of what he said was offensive, more so because it's true. But
true things can *sound* cheapened and distorted when said by people such as Johnson. Trust me on this.

Hmm . . . do I have any ideas as to what you can tell your
parents? A burning desire to see if the sheep on the mainland
are as woolly as the sheep on Skye? The insatiable itch to taste
an English pudding? An urgent need to buy a new hat? An inde-
scribable longing to follow strange American men up to their
hotel rooms?

I'll be leaving in the morning. I wanted to get one more letter off to you before departing Paris, as I'm not sure when I'll
get the chance to mail another. Even though this is what I traveled across the ocean for, I can't help but feel the twinge of
nerves. We will see what tomorrow will bring!

    Your Davey

Isle of Skye
22 January 1916

My dear Davey,

Here I am, back on my little island. Chrissie had to forward
on your letter, hence the delay.

Willie is off to join the rest of you in your silly battles. You
should have seen him strutting around in his uniform, a right
cock o' the walk. The ladies seem to find the kilt nigh on irre-
sistible, but Willie is mystified as to how the men are really expected to work and fight in the ridiculous things.

Over tea, he confided to me that he had a girl. He hadn't
breathed a word to any of us! Though he wouldn't tell me why,
he'd been keeping the whole thing a secret. I let slip that I had a
secret too. I didn't say more than that, but Willie, he deduced
the rest. He said I've been smiling for months. Oh, Davey, I
didn't realise how unprepared I was to answer questions about
us, so I blurted out, "We can't help who we love." He just
grinned and said I was exactly right. I haven't seen him that
happy since the war began.

It is odd to be back here, for so many reasons. My parents'
cottage seems so dim and smoky, the night so much darker and
quieter than I've been used to, and the people grubbier. Although London and Edinburgh had their fair share of dirt (how
can you have that many horses in one city and *not* have it be
dirty?), it was overshadowed by all of that urban sophistication.
Màthair handed me the milking pail right after I arrived, and I
reluctantly changed from trim suit into itchy wool blouse and
sagging skirt, traded my silk stockings and buttoned boots for

hand-knitted stockings and great, clumsy boots. I feel as if there are two Elspeths: One who wears expensive, stylish clothes, travels in taxicabs, dines on duck, and goes across the country on a whim to meet handsome young Americans. And the other, who wears broken-in homemade clothes, travels by shank's mare, dines on porridge, and goes across the country on a whim to meet handsome young Americans.

Remember all of those stories you concocted for me to tell my parents to explain my disappearance? As it turns out, none was needed. As amazing as it may seem, Davey, my mother knew all along! I walked through the door, a dozen stories prepared. Màthair looked up from her spinning and said, "So you went to finally meet your American?" I just about fainted.

Do you remember when I told you how, after Iain left and I was living alone, I would pull out your old letters to read at night? I would sometimes fall asleep literally covered in your words. I was quite the wraith, sometimes not going out of the cottage for days, except to milk and bring in the peats.

One morning I was woken by my mother coming through the front door, stirring up the fire, putting on the kettle. She had brought a big pot of mutton stew with her to warm up for my dinner and spooned some into a bowl for me to take to old Curstag Mór, who lived nearby. When I returned, the floor was swept, the sheets were airing, and the stew was bubbling on the fire. I had left your letters scattered all over the bed and they had been neatly put away, although I didn't think anything of it at the time. I was too in awe of the pot of real food over my fire to worry about wee details like that!

Obviously, Màthair had read the whole stack of letters. I'm

not sure how much she knows—after all, back then we were nothing more than friendly correspondents—but she gave me no censure. It was just that word "finally" that made me wonder how much she really divined from those early letters.

Of course, by insisting that Johnson didn't say anything worth repeating, you've piqued my curiosity even more. Do we really have secrets from each other, Davey? Have we ever had secrets from each other? We've told each other things from the very beginning that our own parents and siblings didn't know. You needn't worry about protecting me from any language or sentiments. This is wartime, you forget. We women are made of sterner stuff these days.

    E

P.S. Minna sent the picture of us that she took outside the register's office. Have you seen it?

Chapter Fourteen

～

Margaret

Glasgow
22 August

Dear Margaret,

It was no impulsive war marriage. Elspeth was married to my best mate, Iain. The three of us had grown up on the hills of Skye. We ran bare-legged down the braes, splashed along the shingle in search of stones. Truth be told, Iain was always a little afraid of Elspeth. Her hair wild, she'd shout poems into the ocean spray. She was as fey as the island. One day we were dangling over the Fairy Bridge and he asked for her hand. She looked at me, then smiled and said yes. I thought the three of us would always be together. I never thought Elspeth would betray him.

As much as I'd like to help, I don't have the answers. I left Skye about a year before you were born. But my màthair, she was there. Write to her on Skye. Your grandmother will know more than I do.

    Finlay

On the train to Fort William
Saturday, 24 August 1940

Dear Paul,

    I'm done with writing letters. I'm on my way to the Isle of Skye!

    Of course, Uncle Finlay didn't give me an address for my grandmother, and I didn't think I'd get far wandering the island, asking the way to "Granny Macdonald's" house. I would imagine that half of Skye is called Macdonald. So I poked around the house looking (again) for a forgotten envelope, an old address book, my mother's birth certificate. Nothing. Not even one of the letters Gran sent each and every month, covered with scribbles of Gaelic. David's letters must be the only ones Mother kept.

    Then I remembered how, from the moment I learned to read, my mother insisted I write my name and address on the inside covers of my books, in case I was to accidently leave a treasured Stevenson or Scott on a park bench. I went at once to her library and pulled the most battered, ancient-looking thing I could find off the shelf, a scruffy copy of *Huckleberry Finn* with a faded poppy pressed in the middle. Sure enough, right inside the cover she'd scrawled "Elspeth Dunn, Seo a-nis, Skye, United Kingdom." As though, even there and then, there was a danger of thieving park benches.

I asked around until I found a family looking to evacuate a child north. Emily's neighbour, Mrs. Calder, has been terrified with all the recent bombings. She's arranged for me to escort her daughter Dorothy to a farm outside Fort William. It pays my fare that far, and it's only a short way from Fort William to Skye. I borrowed a suitcase from Emily and away I went!

I tell you, Paul, this is a little thrilling. Of course it isn't the first time I've been away from Edinburgh but, apart from that jaunt down to Plymouth to see you, I've never been away on my own purposes. Even when you and I went bouldering or rambling the hills, we never went far from the city. Of course, it could be argued that I'm not heading to Skye for myself; I'm heading there for my mother. And the grandmother I've never met! But if I can learn more about Mother's "first volume," about that part of her from before I was born, then the trip will be worthwhile in more ways than one. She's not here to stop me from finding out about my father.

Train to Mallaig
Later

Dear Paul,

Dorothy is settled. A silver-haired woman built like a battleship met us at the station and took charge of both Dorothy and the envelope of money from Mrs. Calder. Before she left, Dorothy pressed a note into my hand, written on the back of her train ticket, and asked me to give it to her mother when I return to Edinburgh. I can scarcely read it for the smudges and tearstains and deplorable penmanship, but it says, "I love you," over and over. She'd folded it over and upon itself a half dozen times and scrawled their address on the front. I promised her it would be the first thing I'd do when arriving back in Edinburgh.

Really, though, I'm starting to worry about Mother—and, I have to admit, feeling somewhat guilty. Maybe it wasn't the letters or the bomb that ran her off. Maybe it was our argument. Even though I've pushed her before to find out who my father is, we've never actually argued. I've always let her shrug it off. I went too far, I asked too much, and I can't help but feel that something fractured in that instant.

Was she right, Paul? Are we rushing into things? Not too long ago, you and I were just friends. We never did anything more serious than offer each other a sandwich or a hand-up on a boulder. When you joined up and asked me if I'd write to you, I almost laughed. I didn't think you and I had enough words between us for letters. Then you said you'd fallen in love, and I thought maybe we did and maybe it could work. But, as my mother said, emotions run high and sharp in wartime. I trust yours—honestly I do—but don't know if I believe my own.

Maybe this trip will be what I need. A lick of independence, a thread of distance. A chance to figure out if this is really what I want. Perhaps this is a journey to solve more than one mystery.

    Affectionately,

    Margaret

London, England
10 August 1940

Dear Sir or Madam,

Many years ago, two men named David Graham and Harry
Vance lived at this address. I do not know if they still stay there
or if they have moved from Chicago, but I would appreciate any
information you could supply. I have been out of touch for some
years and would dearly like to find them.

If you have any information about their whereabouts, can
you please contact me? You can write to me at the Langham
Hotel, London. I thank you in advance.

Sincerely,

Mrs. Elspeth Dunn

Chapter Fifteen

~

Elspeth

—————— , France
February 2, 1916

I'm in———— right now, en route to———. I didn't think it would take so long to get here from Paris. We rode in a freight car and had to stop more times than I could count. I remember making nearly the same trip years ago on a holiday in France but in a plushy first-class car, drinking wine and watching the countryside. This time I was crouched in a freight car, wedged in with my duffel, passing around a flask of execrable brandy. Peering out through the slats of the car, I could recognize some of the stations we passed, although none of the villages looked quite the way I remembered.

The station here is quiet, the streets thronged with men in blue and khaki rather than the gaily dressed holiday-goers from an earlier time. We'll be here for a few more days before moving on. The section we're joining has been *en repos* at————, cleaning and repairing the ambulances, and has been making its way to————. A guy by the name of Pliny, a veteran ambulance driver of sorts who has been away on furlough, is waiting to go up the line with Quinn and me. He told us to enjoy the pastries and hot baths while we could, because it will be awhile before we see either again.

So you insist on knowing what it was that Johnson said to me? He tried all of the usual jokes as to why I might not be joining them in their skirt-chasing. He kept going until he saw my jaw tighten, and then he knew he'd hit on something. "So that's it. Screwing another man's wife, is it? He's out there in Hell's Half Acre and you're back at home—" Well, I won't repeat the rest, as it isn't fit for a lady to read. Let me just say that the comments went downhill from there.

Now you can see why I went after him. His words hurt, not only in what he said but in how he said it. What we did, Sue, what we have, has never seemed wrong to me. Maybe it's easier for me to feel this way. I'm not the one who's married. I don't know your husband. It's easier for me to forget he even exists.

Did the fact that you were married give me pause at the beginning? I would be lying if I said it didn't. I hesitated, Sue. Why do you think it took me so long to tell you I loved you, even when I would've sworn from the hints sprinkled through your letters that you felt the same? You forget, I was raised a good Catholic boy. Despite my wayward childhood, the Ten Commandments are not something I take lightly.

But you said you loved me too. I trusted that you knew what you were doing when you responded. My hesitations melted.

Then we met, we talked, we touched. Any remaining doubts I had floated away. How could something that felt so right be wrong? Everything was perfect. Everything *is* perfect. I've held those memories—those delicate, beautiful memories—close to my heart. And I haven't given much thought to your husband or the tangled mess that is our future.

Until Christmas Eve, when Johnson said what he said, cheapening *us*, Sue. It's impossible to hear disparaging comments like that and not start to believe them after a while, especially when you know they're based in truth. I am "screwing another man's wife." It was a rude reminder of who I was and what I was doing.

It made me wonder how you really felt. You've never mentioned pangs of guilt or feelings of uncertainty. I didn't want to tell you what Johnson said because . . . well, I didn't want you to feel guilty. I didn't want you to reconsider.

The decision has always been yours, Sue, and it still is. You decide whether you want to continue this relationship. You decide where you want to go from here.

Whatever you resolve, know that I am ever . . .

    Your Davey

Isle of Skye
9 February 1916

My dear,

Your letter had more holes in it than a thatched roof in springtime. Either you thought your wee letter needed a bit of ventilation on its long journey to Skye or someone didn't want you to be telling me where you were going or how you got there. With the exception of "France," all other place names were excised.

Am I offended by what Johnson said? Who wouldn't be offended at such language. Am I surprised, though? Not really. When you refused to tell me, I guessed it was something like that.

No, this hasn't been easy for me, although I've tried not to let on just how hard it has been. You're at the front, dealing with the tangled and bloody aftereffects of the war every day. This is my own private war, Davey, and I didn't think you needed to deal with my tangled and bloody conscience.

When you sent me that letter, the one telling me exactly how you felt, I couldn't sleep. I lay awake for nights grappling with my heart. The feelings I have for you are so sharp and so new. But, although my feelings for Iain have changed, they're still there. He's my husband. I can't so easily dismiss either the way I felt or the vows we had made.

Iain is Finlay's best mate. As lads, they were never out of each other's sight. I grew up with Iain always around. When it came time to marry, he seemed the only logical choice. Finlay was over the moon when I said yes to Iain. But things changed. Our paths diverged. My poetry was published and I yearned for the literary lifestyle. I wanted to travel, study, find someone else who'd actually read and understood Lewis Carroll. Iain wanted nothing more than to go about his life the way he had always done. I would go to the beach and look out over the water, wishing I could be anywhere but here. He would go off in his boat with Finlay, knowing that when he returned, I would still be there.

Something wasn't right, even before I got your first letter, Davey. We were floating apart, buoyed by different ambitions and expectations. In you, I found a like-minded soul. You were listening to what I had to say; Iain didn't seem to hear. Then the war started and Iain withdrew completely from my life.

Really, Davey, I don't understand it. He was never so distant when he was here but, now that he's gone at the front, I rarely hear from him. I know what's going on from the newspapers, from Finlay, from the other letters our Skye boys send home. I just don't hear any of this from Iain himself. I don't know if it's something I've done, but he's closed himself off from me. This has always been his reaction—he withdraws rather than face whatever is bothering him.

I didn't plan to fall in love with someone else. I also didn't plan for my husband to leave me without so much as an explanation. I didn't plan any of it, but it happened and I can't say I am unhappy.

I do love you, Davey. And I know this is my decision. Call me an idealist, but I can't help but think that things happen for a reason. You came into my life at the same time that Iain was walking out. You were there for me right when he was not. That has to count for something.

I tell you, it's hard being back in my parents' cottage, back on this tiny island, for all sorts of reasons. I feel so . . . on display. Màthair knows about you and me, and I'm not sure who else does. So many nights, I want to be alone with my thoughts and memories, to lie down and have those sweating, shuddering dreams of you. Just when I start remembering and my pulse quickens, I'll hear my da snore or Finlay cry out in his sleep, and the moment is lost. The cottage isn't big enough for the three of them and for my dreams and me.

E

Place One
February 16, 1916

Sue,

Yep, the censors got to me! They went ahead and sent off the letter anyway (after copious slashing), but I got called to task and reminded of the rules under threat of never being allowed to write to you again. If the letter falls into enemy hands, they don't want to let out where we are, where we're going, or when we might possibly be at either place. As if the Boches don't know exactly where we're at right now. They're peering over the sandbags at the French Army as I write this!

I've finally settled here at "Place One" (I'll be a good boy and stay mysteriously vague). We got in a few days after the rest of the section. The three of us pulled in at night, while many of the rest were on duty. Some were at the picket post in a village not more than a kilometer from the trenches, a twenty-four-hour duty. We were shown to a long building, where we scrounged for a spot in the center of the room, then fell onto our sleeping rolls. I was sleeping so soundly I didn't hear when the first wave of guys trickled in during the night after finishing their runs. Didn't notice a thing until the next morning, when I was beaned in the head by a ball of socks and woke to find Harry grinning at me from the foot of my bed. He had been away at the picket post all night and had just been relieved, only to come in to the barrack and find me curled up in his spot.

I've been assigned an ambulance with a guy they call Riggles, a quiet ex-football player with a perpetual cigarette hanging between his lips. The only time he says a word is when he's exchanging the extinguished stub for a freshly lit one. Riggles has been here almost since the beginning of the American Field Service, so I suppose I couldn't have been paired with anyone better to show me the ropes.

They threw me right into work when I arrived. We've been running evacuation routes, transporting wounded men (charmingly called *blessés*) from dressing stations to hospitals farther behind the line. Most of the dressing stations are at least a few kilometers from the line, so we don't see much aside from the distant smoke of bursting shells.

A few nights ago there was some fierce fighting near here. One of the *blessés* I had was in rough shape. He had been behind a wall when a shell hit and was nearly crushed by the crumbling masonry. I had to drive pretty carefully until I got to the picket post, but, once I passed that and the roads were comparatively smoother, I drove hell-for-leather back to the hospital. A medic said another five minutes and the patient probably would've been lost. It wasn't much, but it was a quiet affirmation of what I am doing here in France.

Okay, Sue, if you promise to stop worrying about me, I'll do the same. I understand why you did what you did. Your love is

too precious for me to push aside just when you need someone
to accept it.

I've been waiting for chow to be served, and I can see the
men starting to line up, so I'll have to cut this short. I think I can
still get it out today.

As tired as I am, Sue, my dreams are always of you.

Love,

Your Davey

Isle of Skye

23 February 1916

My darling boy,

I am sorry for doubting you and the reasons you joined the
Field Service. You're right, Davey, this is something you can do,
and you've already proven in the fortnight you've been there
that you can do it well. There is a big difference between rushing out with a bayonet, intent on maiming or killing, and chan-
neling all of that reckless energy into saving lives. I said before
that you were still a boy, but I think that in a few short months
you've proved yourself to be a man among men.

Please keep yourself warm, happy, and, as always, safe.

E

Place One
March 2, 1916

Sue,

I'm on a chow foraging run, which means I get a chance for a
bath and a real meal while I'm here in town. I'm lingering probably longer than necessary over my omelet, because it gives me
the chance to write to you before I have to get back in my flivver.

Harry and I both managed to be *en repos* the other day, something that doesn't often happen, as we end up working most
every day, even when we are due a day off. We each brought
books and a pitiful little picnic—tins of "meat," crackers, a tiny
raisin cake Minna sent, washed down with a bottle of perfect
swill that was quite obviously mislabeled "wine." I sincerely
think that, after washing out his socks, Pliny refilled the bottle
with the wash water, as that is precisely what it tasted like. Despite the vile wine and the equally vile canned beef (or was it
cat?), it was a pleasant afternoon. I got *Tarzan of the Apes* nearly
finished. I only wish I could've devoured my picnic with the
same relish!

We actually had quite a feast a few days ago. One of the men
received the Croix de Guerre and threw a banquet to mark the
occasion. He spared no expense and brought in a Parisian chef.
Real food, wine that deserved to be called French wine, and all
of it off china and linen. I swear, Sue, I felt too grimy to approach such an elegant spread, but approach I did, and we all
tucked in before you could say "Yankee Doodle Dandy." Truly,

Sue, it was a spread that would've done Ranhofer or Escoffier proud.

My mouth is starting to water again at the memory, so please excuse any drips and smudges of the ink. And to think I just finished eating! Ah . . . the memory of that meal: That will keep us psychologically fed through many weeks of boiled beef and turnip soup.

> Love you,
> David

Isle of Skye
14 March 1916

Oh, Davey,

I don't know what to feel anymore.

Iain's gone missing.

I only just got the letter from the War Office, and I'm not even sure it's sunk in. I read the words, I cried out once, but since then I haven't said a thing—as though by ignoring it, I could make it go away. Missing. How could that be?

Finlay's an absolute wreck. He kept repeating, "I wasn't there. I couldn't help him," then walked out of the cottage. He limped back late that night, filthy and missing his cane, and slept for two days straight. It was up to me to tuck him into bed, patch up his torn trousers, find a length of wood for another cane. He's useless without it.

I want to know: Why is Finlay allowed to collapse? Why do

I have to be the one to stay strong and pick up the pieces? Nobody else has. Iain is *my* husband. I'm the one who should feel this weighing more than anyone. I'm the one who should be so crushed I can barely breathe.

You know I'm not very devout. I'm not a regular churchgoer. When I'm out on the mountain all by myself, I feel closer to God. It's almost pagan, though, so far away from the hymns and sermons. Now I'm thinking I've neglected something vital. I didn't give God his proper due and then I teased him with my infidelities, and now Iain is being punished for my sins.

Maybe I have made the wrong decision. I don't know what to think anymore. If I were to stop, would that bring him back?

Elspeth

Place Three
March 21, 1916

Sue,

Have you had any news?

"Missing" could mean a lot of things. It could mean nothing. Until you hear more, don't speculate. Please.

I've heard the guys in the back of my flivver talk about it enough. One minute you're hunkered down, sharing a cigarette, the next you're up and over the trench wall and into No Man's Land. Close to seventy pounds on your back, running with bayonet fixed, dodging shell holes, debris, your pals. Everything's so covered in mud you could run right over your own brother and not recognize him. You can't even stop to take a second look, much less drag anyone to safety. Iain could be lying out there hurt, waiting for the stretchers to bring him back. He could've been lost in the rush over the wall. Don't think of only the worst.

Sue, you have enough to worry about right now without adding guilt and divine chastisement to it all. Yes, I believe in God. I've always attended church, even during my hoyden college days; I just had more to admit to in the confessional back then.

When I was younger, Evie and I had a book of Bible stories, a lovely illustrated volume we would pore over on lazy Sunday afternoons. I remember one picture of God from that book. He was shown as a serene personage with a snowy white beard and rosy cheeks—looking not too unlike Santa Claus, now that I think of it—gazing down on the newly created world with pride. It reminded me of the way a father might look on a newborn child. I've always held that picture in my mind, and I think that's why I could never believe in a vengeful God. That kindly, fatherly figure could never blame me for being led astray. He could never turn from me because of my minor transgressions.

Think for a moment, Sue. With all of the atrocities the kaiser is committing, with all of the fighting and killing going on over here, do you really think God is looking down and directing his anger at a woman whose only sin is having too much love to give?

I'm so tired right now. Just got off twenty-four-hour duty and have hardly had more than a few hours of snatched sleep.

But I didn't want to put off writing to you. If I can't be there (epistolarily, at least) when you need me, then what point is there in me being with you at all?

You may have noticed from the heading that we've moved again. There was a Place Two between then and now, but we didn't stay for more than a few days. We're a bit closer to the line this time but not close enough that we have to worry about shells falling in on us while we sleep—which is good because, with the hours that we keep, we need all of the sleep we can get.

And on that note, Sue, I'm going to go to bed. I can barely hold the pencil as it is. Please keep me updated. Despite the circumstances, I truly do care. I wish I could be there to hold you, but this is the best that I can do.

I do love you, my girl.

David

Isle of Skye
28 March 1916

David,

How could I *not* worry? How could I not think the absolute worst?

I've received a letter from a man in Iain's battalion, a Private Wallace. He said he went over the top with Iain that day. He lost track of him in the fighting. When the retreat sounded, Private Wallace ran back and passed Iain on the way, "badly wounded." Iain was so bad off that he couldn't make his way back to the British trench, even when Private Wallace offered a shoulder to help. It was some time before any stretcher-bearers could work their way up there. Even with the approximate location given to them by Private Wallace, the stretcher-bearers said that they couldn't find anyone. Not anyone needing a doctor's care, that is.

Finlay is beside himself. He and Iain were to watch out for each other. He blames himself for not being there to keep an eye on Iain. He blames himself for not bringing Iain home.

It's easy for you to say that God isn't punishing me, but you're not going through the private hell I am. You aren't feeling the anguish and guilt I'm feeling. How do you *know* I'm not being punished in some way? All Iain asked for was my love, and I couldn't even give him that wholeheartedly. Perhaps that's my sin. Perhaps that's what I'm being punished for.

Yes, I know you really care how I'm feeling, but, admit it, you also have your own self-interests to protect. You don't want me moping about and brooding over my missing husband. But maybe moping is what I need to do. Maybe moping shows that I'm looking for some redemption.

　　Elspeth

Isle of Skye
12 April 1916

David,

I didn't mean you should stop writing to me. Your letters are still one of the few things keeping me afloat. Remember that whole "sea of chaos" bit?

Maybe I sounded angry in my last letter. I know you really do care. I'm just confused, Davey. I'm confused and I'm being confronted by those feelings of guilt. Then I feel guilty that I wasn't feeling guilty before. Does that make any sense?

Also, I'm worried. Regardless of what I feel for you, Iain is my husband and I will always love him. I can't bear to think of him in pain or distress.

And I'm uncertain. I don't know how I want this all to turn out. Of course I want Iain to be safe and well. But there's a small evil part of me, a part I keep trying to ignore, looking at all of this with some measure of relief—at not having to make any decisions in the end, at not having to be uncertain any longer. Then I feel guilty once again for being so uncertain.

Please write back, Davey. I miss you.

E

Isle of Skye
22 April 1916

Davey,

Where are you? Why haven't you written? I don't know what I could've said to turn you away. Wherever you've gone, please come back to me. I don't know what I would do without you.

Where are you, Davey?

Sue

Isle of Skye
25 April 1916

Don't do this to me! For the love of God, I can't lose you
too! Is everyone I love destined to disappear?

I'm not strong enough for this, Davey. I can't do it all on my
own without knowing you exist in this world. I need you as I
need breath in my body.

I will pray to whatever god I have to if it will bring you back
to me. I will pray to the fairies and imps that inhabit my island.
I will pray to you, in the Temple of my Heart.

Oh, my love! My love.

Chapter Sixteen

~

Margaret

Portree, Skye
Tuesday, 27 August 1940

Dear Paul,

It's raining on Skye. It's been raining since the ferry docked. I told the ferry captain I'm from Edinburgh; I'm used to precipitation. He just chuckled and chewed the stem of his pipe.

Portree curls around the harbour, soft and smudged, like a chalk painting left out in the rain. Of course, I didn't bring an umbrella—who in Edinburgh really carries an umbrella?—so I had to dart through the drizzle with my suitcase held above my head until I found a pub to duck into. Now I'm tucked by a fire, steaming and drowsy, with a hot toddy and that tattered old book. Staring at the address that's not really an address. No street name or house number. Elspeth Dunn, Seo a-nis, Skye, United Kingdom.

I know I should get up, perhaps go find the post office to ask about the address, but it's too warm here by the fire. The rain is still pattering on the glass. Maybe I'll order another and keep warm a while longer.

A moment ago, I was content to sit in here all day, waiting out the rain, but now I'm stirred to action! Just as I was writing to you about being content by the peat fire, I overheard the surly publican chatting with the dowagers at the next table in a language I know from my mother's lullabies.

"Is that Gaelic you're speaking?" I asked. When they nodded, I held out the book. "Please, what does 'Seo a-nis' mean?" I won't tell you how I attempted to pronounce it. You'd be heartily disappointed in me. I'm sure both of the women were.

But instead of translating, the taller of the two women pointed at the scrawl and exclaimed, "Elspeth Dunn! That's a name I haven't heard in quite some time."

The other nodded. "She left years ago."

"Seo a-nis is her house. She still owns it, doesn't she?"

"The family does."

I had no idea what I thought I'd find at my mother's old house. Bits and pieces of the past? I only knew I had to go. "Where is it?"

And, can you believe it, they looked me up and down! The publican smirked. "It's more than a stroll, miss."

Miss? Really.

"I'm no stranger to walking," I'm afraid I said, somewhat stiffly. "If you can please point me in the right direction."

"It's out towards Peinchorran." He leaned on the table. "I can sell you a map and a compass. And an umbrella."

I took him up on the map—marked for her house in pencil—and the compass. Right now I'm hunched in the doorway of the post office, finishing this letter to you and wishing I'd also taken him up on the brolly. The rain is still coming in fits and starts, but there's no car to take me down to her house. A bit over eight miles. We've done close to that before! I've changed into my oxfords and intend to attempt it. My mother has a house on the Isle of Skye. Rain or no rain, I plan to find it!

    Margaret

27 August 1940

Dear Maisie,

I'm crossing my fingers and mailing this to you care of your mother's old address on Skye, as it's all I have. With luck, it will find its way to you.

From the moment we met, you've been wondering where you came from. The wheres and hows and whys of Margaret Dunn. Just be chary. Not that every father is a skiver like mine, but I don't want you to be disappointed. I've heard you talk about who your father could be. An earl? A general? Basil Rathbone? You didn't have "island crofter" on that list.

But isn't that what searching for the past is? Surprising, shocking, perhaps even a wee bit scary. We never know what we'll find. But I know you need to at least look. You'll never know if you're on the right course for your life until you see the course that has brought you to where you are today.

You wondered if we were rushing things, if we could trust the way we felt. My sweet lass, I wouldn't push you into anything you're unsure about. By all means, consider as long as you wish. But answer me this: The moment you said "yes" and took my hand, what were you feeling?

For me, I felt as if my heart would jump straight out of my chest, and I've kept ahold of that. Every time I start to remember standing chest-deep in the water off Dunkirk, not knowing if the planes would miss me, not knowing if I'd ever make it onto a ship, I'd think of your hand in mine and then any worries would melt away. Of all the things in the world right now, the way I feel about you is the one thing that I *do* trust.

Take care and write me as soon as you can.

Love,
Paul

Beagan Mhìltean, Skye
Friday, 30 August 1940

Dear Paul,

I did set off to look for Seo a-nis that same rainy day I arrived. Which, in retrospect, was a bit of a mistake. Much of my walk there was cross-country (though, I do admit, this was probably due to my poor map-reading skills more than anything else). And it was no flower-strewn Borders path. I went up and down rises, across desolate stretches, with no one but sheep for company. Although I had my oxfords on, they were no match for the mud of Skye. I don't know how many times I had to hop back to extract a shoe. I'd brought my suitcase (though any sensible person would've left it back in town), because I thought to change into something dry once I arrived, though I soon saw what a fruitless idea that was. My suitcase was soaked straight through. I tucked the whole in the lea of a crumbling stone fence to come back for later. I still haven't found it.

I finally passed an old man walking a dog towards Portree (at least I think so; I swear, the compass must be defective). He reassured me that I was on Peinchorran and pointed the way to Seo a-nis. He said it was the only thing along that edge of the loch and I couldn't miss it. He was right.

It didn't look as if anyone had been in the cottage in decades. It's one of those white, lime-washed buildings you see all over here, with two up and two down, and a chimney on either end. A real slate roof, though many of the tiles had fallen over the years. The shutters were nailed tight and boards stretched across. I tried the door, but it had warped and wouldn't budge a hair.

Next to the cottage was an older one, a low stone building with a rotted thatch roof. Beyond that, a tumbled fence marked off an overgrown garden, nothing much more than thistles at this point. Everything was quiet, apart from the waves crashing against the shingle and the bleating of distant sheep.

The rain had slowed to a misty drizzle. I thought to walk down to the beach, to see if I could find any other sign of life. As I skirted the side of the house, I sent up a roosting flock of

something feathered from the half-thatched building. I turned
the corner and, oh, Paul, I froze.

The whole back of the cottage, the side facing out to the sea,
glowed with colour. It was like an Italian fresco, caught in the
Hebrides. The lime-washed wall was covered with whorls and
curves of paintings, some straight out of the Gaelic legends and
lullabies Mother would rock me to sleep with. Selkie women
slipping from their sealskins on the beach. A ring of fairies
dancing around a shuddering green flame. A woman dressed in
rose petals on top of a crag, her tears running down to the sea.
The pictures merged and overlapped. A couple waltzing. A
bowl of oranges. A pink pearl gleaming within an open oyster.
Then images I knew could have come only from the last war.
An ambulance hurtling past an explosion, while rows of boys
marched by. The driver of the ambulance leaned out the window, his face tilted towards the loch, and I swear there was a
gleam in his brown-green eyes.

"She painted all that," said a voice behind me. "During the
Great War, when she was waiting."

The woman was small and neat, with black eyes as sharp as a
crow's. Behind her, an ancient truck rumbled.

"I heard that someone in Portree was asking after Elspeth
Dunn."

All I could do was nod.

"And those fools sent you here." She tightened a shawl over
her shoulders. "You'd better come with me."

She reached for my arm, but I stiffened. It had been a long
day.

"Och, you have Elspeth's spirit. She always had a set to her mou as a lass. I see the same in you, Margaret Dunn." I must have shown surprise, because her eyes softened suddenly and she smiled. "I'm your gran. I've been waiting for you."

And here I thought she didn't speak a word of English, any more than she could read or write it. I'd always dismissed her as my Skye gran, too busy on her croft to visit us in Edinburgh. But that didn't mean she didn't care. I told you she wrote letters in Gaelic to my mother every month for as long as I could remember. But, Paul, Mother wrote Gran every *week*, letters covered with crisscrossed lines, telling Gran every step I took, every dream I had, every wish I made before bed. And photographs! My first day of school, my missing front teeth, my tenth birthday, my Confirmation, all taken with Mother's old Challenge folding camera. Gran has kept all of the letters in a kist at the foot of her bed, with the pictures tacked inside the lid. Although she was far from Edinburgh, she was never far from us.

I've been this week at my gran's house, meeting a family I didn't know I had and walking the burns and crags, thinking of you. I can't help but think of all the rambles you and I could take here. You'd help me sort through this all, then you'd take my hand, and I'd feel as safe as I did when I said "yes" to you in Plymouth. I don't know what I'd do without you.

Love,
Maisie

London, England
16 August 1940

Dear Sir or Madam,

Many years ago, a woman named Eve Hale, née Graham, lived at this address with her husband and daughter. I do not know if they still stay there or if they have moved from Terre Haute, but I would appreciate any information you could supply. I have been out of touch for some years and would dearly like to find them. Eve is the sister of an old friend of mine.

If you have any information about their whereabouts, can you please contact me? You can write to me at the Langham Hotel, London. I thank you in advance.

Sincerely,

Mrs. Elspeth Dunn

Chapter Seventeen

~

Elspeth

Ste. Geneviève, Paris, France
April 28, 1916

My Sue,

A million and one apologies for not writing more before!
You were probably worried sick when you got nothing but that
hospital postcard I sent, but I wasn't in shape to write much.
I am feeling heaps better now and thought you deserved more
of an explanation.

I was working a route that went to a *poste* near the rear
trench. Close enough to "smell hell," as they say. Due to the
heavy shelling, the *blessés* hadn't yet been brought to this particular *poste*, so I stayed in the dugout, waiting. Pretty soon I saw
the *brancardiers* struggling up over the ridge above the dugout.
This rise is a bit chancy, as it is fully in view of the Boche guns.
It was a moonlit night, and there was a brief moment when the

brancardiers and stretcher were illuminated at the top of the ridge. Long enough for a gunner to open fire.

I saw the stretcher fall and so I ran up the hill. One of the *brancardiers* was down, but the *blessé* seemed to be okay. I pulled the wounded *brancardier* down the hill a ways and then helped the other guy with the stretcher. We were fired upon again. A shell hit quite close, enough to get me with some fragments in the shoulder and right foot. We somehow managed to get the *blessé*, the wounded *brancardier*, and me into the ambulance, though I was in no shape to drive.

My wounds weren't too serious, but I got an infection and was quite feverish. I was moved farther back, until I ended up here in Paris. I'm so sorry, Sue. I know you must've been worried when you got that postcard saying I was in the hospital. I was in no condition to write. The French doctors put tubes in the wound to drain off infection, and I couldn't move my arm for a few weeks. And none of my nurses spoke a word of English, so I couldn't even dictate a letter. My shoulder is still rather sore and I'm writing this in brief stages. In my fevered dreams, though, you were always there, sitting next to me.

Your Davey

P.S. Please, please, please send some books! I'm not sure how much longer I'll be in the hospital, but I am near to climbing the walls for lack of anything interesting to read.

Hôtel République, Paris, France
May 6, 1916

My dear, funny girl! When I asked for books, I intended for
you to just pop them in the mail. Although Louisa May Alcott?
You *did* grab whatever was on hand as you ran out the door.
What I can't figure out, though, is how you could make it
through a ten-plus-hour train ride with nothing aside from *Jo's
Boys* to read. But, really, Sue, that's what you get for dashing
out of the house with absolutely no suitcase! Not even a clean
pair of socks. Good thing I lent you a pair of mine. I know
you'll give them back someday.

You're always in my thoughts, but to see you again in person, drink you up like the sweetest medicine in the whole
hospital—I feel like a new man. The doctors and nurses might
as well have been peddling barley water for all it compared to
you. My own personal tonic.

I'll be heading back to Place Three tomorrow. Will write
more then. I just wanted there to be a letter waiting for you
when you got home.

    Davey

Somewhere in the channel
6 May 1916

Davey, Davey. You didn't have to get yourself shot in order
to get my attention! You know that I love you regardless. It was
a very sneaky ploy to get me onto a boat, though. If I hadn't

seen evidence to the contrary with my own eyes, I never would've believed you were as sick as you suggested.

You looked quite pathetic, dear, stretched out on that hospital cot, that you had me in a grip of worry when I first spotted you! So thin and pale under that sheet, your curls limp on the pillow—I about burst into tears. But then you opened those eyes, the color of the hills, and said, "There you are," as if you'd been expecting me, and I knew you were fine. I'm surprised they discharged you so quickly, but perhaps they wanted to get rid of you after so long. Though after the comments you kept whispering in my blushing ear, I'm not surprised. The nurses are *nuns,* Davey. You're lucky they didn't speak a word of English.

Not that we needed words once in that hotel room. Your kisses very effectively stopped mine, the way they did in London. Very effectively. I wouldn't have wished any of that long, tangled night away for an instant, but, my dearest, if I had known how much pain you would be in the next morning, I might have hesitated. Or, at the very least, bought a second bottle of brandy.

Oh, I wish we could've had more than that night! I wish we could have hidden in that room as long as the last time. Nine days to kiss, eat oranges, have good intentions of sleeping. But I know you had to go check in. I know you had to head back out to that ambulance of yours. To let you go again only half a day after catching you back in my arms—oh, Davey, it was impossibly hard. But you're right. I worry so much about our "tomorrow," about each and every goodbye, that I don't enjoy the "right now."

There's enough to worry about in the future. I have no idea

what tomorrow will tell about Iain. I have no idea what tomorrow will tell about anything. But you sat on that bed, bare-chested and beautiful and *here*. Davey, you are my "right now."

At a time when I feel so uncertain, I was reassured by your confidence. I think seeing you, though, was the only tonic I needed. It cleared away any doubts and worries.

I should get back up to Skye in a few days. I'll go straight through this time, not stopping in Edinburgh. I'll write more once I get home. I just wanted there to be a letter waiting for you at Place Three.

> All my love,
> Sue

Place Three
May 9, 1916

Sue,

Back at Place Three. Found your other letters waiting for me, the ones from the 12th, 22nd, and 25th. Were you really so worried? I'm touched, actually. I should get myself wounded more often. Not only did it work rather well at getting you to forgive me and getting you to admit how much you adore me, but I got the added bonus of seeing your beautiful face once more. And, once you got me out of that bleak hospital, there was the added, *added* bonus, which (to be perfectly honest) probably did my poor battered body more harm than good but left my mind in an oh-so-blissful state.

I'm still not quite up to par, but I'm doing better. They've offered me a citation for my actions. More important (at least in our section) is that I've finally earned my nickname! These nicknames are very important among us, as they signify that you've "proven" yourself and are truly part of the bunch. I've already told you about Pliny and Riggles. Harry already has his nickname—can you believe his real name is Harrington? Among the squad, we also have Lump, Jersey, Skeeter, Gadget, Bucky, and Wart. Don't ask where they all came from, as I'm not sure I could even tell you! I've been christened Rabbit. The guys say I'm so lucky with these scrapes of mine, it's as if I have a lucky rabbit's foot. Not my right foot, of course, but my left foot came out okay, and isn't that the lucky one, anyhow?

Your Lucky Rabbit (always!)

Isle of Skye
15 May 1916

Davey,

You are *not* to get yourself wounded again! Not so much as a sliver in your toe. Do you hear me? If you do, I shan't come down again. I'll toss every letter you send into the grate and ignore your boyish cries for attention.

You didn't tell me: Is it part of your job to hike up dangerous parapets to fetch stretchers? All this time, I consoled myself with thinking you were safe, playing chauffeur well behind the lines. And now you say that you are not only driving right up to the danger zone but *getting out of your vehicle*! Please promise me you won't do that again.

I did finally get the postcard you sent when you first arrived in hospital. Doesn't say much for the mail service that it got here almost a month after you sent it. If I had received that card when I was intended to get it, I would've been to see you even sooner. Curse the General Post Office!

I arrived back here on Skye to find that my new cottage is finished. It probably won't look like much to you, but to me it is a palace. Two storeys, a wooden floor, a chimney on each end of the house, windows with glass, and a door that latches! Such luxuries, I tell you. Here's a wee sketch of the new place.

Finlay has been helping over there, working on the building. Since getting his prosthetic leg, he's gradually been able to find a small measure of peace. Da found some thick pieces of driftwood and Finlay fitted them together in a mantel for my sitting room. He then carved the mantel all the way around with mermaids and selkies and sprites. It is truly the mantel of an island girl. It is the mantel of a girl who has conquered the sea by conquering her fears.

Poor Finlay, though, has been rather melancholy. Iain is not the only one he mourns. Things have been going sour with his girl, Kate. Since he returned, she's been coming by less and less. Finlay's still holding out hope that she'll come back to him, get used to his leg, the way he's had to. But I'm not so sure. Nearly every time I go to the post office, I see her, and with perfume-soaked envelopes. I can't bring myself to tell Finlay. He'd just crumble, Davey.

I am on my way back to my own croft, to start moving things into the cottage. I know the bedding needs a hearty washing and the mattress an airing. Everything else could probably

use a good scrubbing as well before I put it away in the clean
new cottage. I'll post this on my walk over there.

Missing you already,

E

Place Three
May 22, 1916

Sue,

Okay, cross my heart and kiss my elbow. You won't hear
about me doing such stupid things again. I swear. How is that
for an oath?

Things feel different here. I told you before about getting
your nickname as being a rite of passage, to make you one of the
guys. It really did seem to change my relationship with
everyone. The guys have always been friendly to me, but I
wasn't close with anyone aside from Harry. I felt this constant
nagging need to compete and best each and every one of them.
But now I realize we're all on the same side. I might even find a
friend or two.

This is something new for me. I know, I know, hard to believe that with my sparkling personality and unerring sense of
humor I wouldn't be the most popular guy on campus, but I've
always been one of those who has many acquaintances but few
friends. Now I feel the camaraderie I've always read about.

I was reading through some of the Darley poetry last night,
and it struck me that I haven't heard you talk about your poetry
for a while. I know I've been keeping you running from one end

of the country to the other, but have you been able to find time to write?

The other day I scratched off a little fairy story about a princess with a magic traveling crown and mailed it off to Florence, but after I sent it, I counted out and realized she's four years or so now. Is she too old for Uncle Dave's fairy stories? What is it that four-year-old girls like? She is learning to draw and sends me the most frenzied pictures (thankfully accompanied by Hank's written description). The last one was entitled: "Mama and the chickens and Aunt Sally's cat by the seashore."

As I write this, I'm eating my lunch, a rather dismal stew that seems to be mostly turnips and cabbage, and I'm thinking about when we ate at the Carlton. Braised duck, oysters, your first taste of champagne. I can still picture your eyes lighting up at the desserts. I can't believe you ordered one of each! That seems ages ago, although it wasn't more than half a year. Half a year, half a lifetime. Doesn't seem to be much of a difference between the two when you and I are apart.

Do you remember what you said to me when we first met at King's Cross? The very first words you spoke? You glided over to me and, as I was struggling to think of something intelligent to say, you said, "There you are." I often think of that, Sue. Here I am. No matter where I am in the world, "Here I am."

Davey

Isle of Skye
29 May 1916

Davey,

I'm in my cottage and I've embarked on a wee project. With the whole building lime-washed white, it just looked too tempting a canvas, so I've bought up all the pigments I could find in Portree and have been embellishing the outside. I perch myself up on the ladder, with my pockets stuffed full of brushes and jars, a curved piece of driftwood balanced on the roof for a palette, and let my imagination and memories flow through my fingers. I'm sure it looks like nonsense to any passing boat or hikers on the other side of the loch, but it all fits together in my mind. Each swirl of colour, each flick of the brush, is a tribute to us.

Finlay has finished my mantel, and it truly is a work of art. So much care taken, down to the tiniest details. Right in the centre is a fairy princess with a face that looks remarkably like Kate's. I told him he was wasting his time on Skye, that he should be at the Glasgow School of Art, studying sculpture. He shouldn't languish here like me, wasting his art on crofters' cottages. Now that he's off the boats, he's not bound here anymore, the way the rest of us are. He can set off into the world the way we always dreamed as children.

Truth be told, I want him to go from here; I want him to stop thinking about Kate. When I was mailing your last letter, I saw her in the post office. The wind from the open door pulled the letter from her fingers and I caught it for her. Oh, Davey, it was addressed to Willie. The whole thing reeked of cheap perfume.

She saw that I noticed but, uppity minx that she is, turned up her nose and refused to say a word. I probably should have told Finlay right away, told him that Kate had been playing him false all along with his own brother, but, oh, I couldn't. Not when it seemed he was finding some peace with his life at last.

I think he may know already, though. Willie came home on leave last week, strutting like a peacock, regaling us with stories of brave battles, then hurrying off. I caught him outside the cottage, heading towards Portree. I told him I knew about Kate. I knew she was the girl he'd been going around with and that he should stop, for Finlay's sake. He just laughed and said that a husband hadn't stopped me and, anyway, I'd told him there was nothing wrong with following one's heart. That he was only keeping with it because I was doing the same thing. That we were alike.

Davey, what he's doing feels so wrong. And I'm seeing Finlay, broken in pieces over it. Just a few days after, Willie went out to help Finlay on my cottage. He came home with a bloodied nose, and Finlay didn't come home at all until the next day. He must know. How could he ever forgive either of them?

And, according to Willie, I've been doing the same to Iain all along. Thinking about me rather than about him. All of those little fingers of guilt I get every now and again, they came on me full force with Willie's words. Not only was I a sneak and a cheat but I'd led my own brother to do the same. I'd caused a rift in more than my marriage. I'd caused one in my family.

I could've given Willie different advice. I could've told Finlay about Kate's letter back when I had the chance. But I've done nothing, and now my brothers won't speak to each other.

And behind it all are my own actions. If I hadn't done what I did to Iain, Willie never would have felt justified in his decisions. My family would still be whole.

Davey, my love, my boy, it has to stop. I have to stop. And, believe me, my fingers do not want to write these words. But I can't do this anymore to Iain. When he's found, when he comes home, I have to tell him. I have to straighten things out with him before there can be anything with us. Things weren't good between Iain and me; surely he won't disagree. But, Davey, I have to go about this the right way or I may never be able to forgive myself.

That's why I've been painting our story on the side of my cottage. A reminder of what was. A memorial to us in paint and brush.

Please understand. Know that I love you, but please understand.

Elspeth

Place Three
June 8, 1916

Sue,

You don't know how I've been dreading this letter from you. I knew it would be coming someday, but I dreaded it all the same.

The day you wrote back and said that you loved me too, Sue, you turned my world upside down. Life has never looked the same to me since I read those words. But your last letter, that's turned it around again, and I'm dizzier than before. I haven't slept since.

I could beg you not to leave me. That's exactly what the selfish boy in me wants to do. And, deep down, I think that's what you want me to do too. But, all of this I'm doing here, it's an effort to prove myself worthy of you, worthy of whatever it is that we have. That man wouldn't pull you away from those you love. He wouldn't send cracks running through your life.

All I will beg, though, is that you consider for a while longer. Don't shut me out just yet. This has all come so suddenly. I would not hold you in something you do not want, but give me more time. Let me hold you a little while longer. Until Iain returns, please stay with me.

Always,
Davey

Isle of Skye
19 June 1916

Dear Davey,

I received a formal letter from the War Office. As there has been no further news received, Private Iain Dunn is regretfully presumed to have been killed in action.

The moment I heard the knock on the door, I knew. I didn't even open the letter right away, just set it up on the mantel Finlay carved. Funny, my very first thought was of Finlay, how he'd collapse at the news. I had to shore myself up. I had to be there for my brother.

I didn't sleep at all after the letter came. I spent the night in the old cottage, sorting through Iain's few things. He left behind so little, such scant evidence that a man once lived. I couldn't bring myself to move anything from the places he laid them.

Forgotten on a shelf in the old cottage, a nautical almanac from 1910—did he really once read?—and a carved pipe. Evenings, while I sat and scribbled, Iain carved. He got that from Finlay, I know. I still remember the two of them as boys, sitting down by the shore with dark heads bent together, whittling pieces of driftwood into peg dolls and tops for me. In recent years, he'd started fishing in deeper waters, staying out in the boat all night. I told myself it was because he was tired of doing nothing but carving and staring into the fire every evening. Now I just don't know.

He kept a small kist for his clothes, though he walked out the door wearing most all that he owned. Nothing left in the kist but two oft-mended blue shirts I made when we first married. They were enthusiastically uneven, but he never complained, only brought them to me for mending when the old patches wore out. I still have a length of that blue fabric somewhere. Amazing that the shirts lasted longer than we did.

Tucked in the back of the kist was a broken wooden comb. He always wore his hair too long. He said he liked to feel it blowing against his forehead when he was out on the water. The night before he left, he sat in front of the fire in just his trousers and cut his hair short. I thought to catch it all up and tuck the locks between the pages of Byron, but he tossed it all into the fire. I wasn't that sentimental, anyhow.

At the bottom of the kist, I found a dented biscuit tin, crusted with salt and rusted shut. It must've lived in his seabag, before he emptied it and packed for the army. I had to lever it open with the meat knife. And, oh, Davey! Inside, a copy of my first book, *Waves to Peinchorran*. We hadn't been married yet when I gave it to him, not knowing if he'd ever read it. The pages were water-stained and, right in the middle, at a poem about summer nights, was a twisted lock of my hair. In pencil he'd underlined the phrase "warm as a breath on my face." Next to the book was a carved wooden baby rattle.

Since then I've been sitting here, wrapped in a sweater of his, staring into the fire. Màthair came over yesterday and clucked her tongue to see me sweltering in front of a fire with a wool sweater. She brought in water for a bath and set to work making a fish pie. While the pie cooked, she helped me wash my hair and asked, "Is it guilt you're feeling?"

How could I explain to her that it wasn't guilt over loving you, that it was guilt over not loving Iain enough? That all this time I spent thinking he was turning from me, he wasn't. He went away, chasing herring up the Minch, but he carried a piece of me with him. He always kept me close.

I feel so hollow, Davey. Back when I got the other letter, when I found out he'd gone missing, I told myself he was dead. I cried my allotment of tears then. Why would I tell myself anything different? Hope is useless at a time like that. Hope only sets you up for disappointment.

Davey, I don't know how to do this. Mourn. I didn't shed a tear when the letter arrived, and I still haven't. I can't leave the house, because who would understand? There goes his widow, who refuses to cry. There goes his widow, who doesn't care.

But I do. He was my husband. How could I not care?

I don't know what it is I expect you to say. I'm not entirely sure why I'm writing, except that's what I do. Màthair told me not to stop. She told me to keep writing "my American," that there was no better way to keep me going.

Please don't leave me, Davey.

Sue

Chapter Eighteen

⁓

Margaret

Beagan Mhìltean, Skye
Saturday, 31 August 1940

Dear Paul,

   After Gran found me at Seo a-nis and brought me back to her house, she could see the questions in my eyes. But she put me off. Told me we could talk tomorrow. She had a big pot of brose cooking over a fire and set me down at the table across from my grandfather and my uncle Willie, two men as weathered as the Crags. Gran kept those sharp crow's eyes fixed on me, but Grandfather didn't look at much but the inside of his eyelids the whole meal.

   With no sounds but the crackling of the fire and the scraping of spoons in bowls, I waited for Gran to say something. Such a wee woman, yet so intimidating. She'd dried me off and given me an ancient sweater and a pair of Grandfather's trousers to put on. My own clothes steamed quietly in front of the fire. Uncomfortable in strange clothes in a strange place, I waited for Gran to go first.

Uncle Willie blethered the whole meal, with anecdotes about Skye, questions about Edinburgh, and a whole string of awful jokes. About himself or my mother, he said nothing. From Gran's tight mouth and narrowed eyes, I gathered that Willie was the family disappointment. Unmarried, uncouth, still taking up space in her house.

Through all Willie's talk, Gran sat silently, watching me. A battle of wills, and the old woman was the more stubborn of us. I finally broke and asked her how she knew I'd be coming. On a place such as Skye, I could full well believe in second sight.

"Finlay wrote to me."

Willie's spoon clattered into his bowl. "Finlay wrote?"

"First time in twenty or so years." She had a glint of satisfaction in her eyes. "He said Elspeth's daughter had tracked him down and, if she stayed as persistent, would be up on my doorstep in no time."

"Why didn't you tell me he wrote?"

Gran glared. "Just because you live in my house and eat my bread does not mean I tell you everything, Willie Macdonald."

Willie didn't even look chagrined. "He's my brother."

"And yet he didn't write to you."

Willie thumped back his chair and, with no apology, left the kitchen.

Disappointment indeed. My first night there, and already in the middle of a family squabble.

"Finlay wrote that you were asking about Elspeth when she

was younger," Gran said. "That you wanted to know your mother before you were born."

I nodded. "He wouldn't tell me much."

"Finlay's as stubborn as Elspeth, to be sure. All these years, both of them waiting for the other to apologise." She scraped the last of the brose from the pot into my bowl. "Both were more alike than they'd ever admit, even as children. They were our dreamers, the two never content with a crofting life. Both were starving for knowledge. They read and reread everything they could reach. Both kept their eyes on the horizon, as though looking for a way to touch it. Both, when they gave their hearts away, lost them for good."

I remember exactly what she said, because I made her repeat it and then scribbled it down the moment I could.

"The difference, though, was that the poetry was only in Finlay's soul. It was in Elspeth's very fingertips." She gathered in the bowls and stacked them with a clatter. "To bed with you, Margaret Dunn. In the morning I will give you that 'first volume.'"

Those black eyes didn't brook any argument, and I knew where Mother had got her stubbornness.

When I woke in the morning, the cottage was quiet, everyone having gone off to their chores around the croft. On the kitchen table rested a plate of fresh bannocks, a pot of jam, and a tall stack of gilt-edged poetry books. All written by my mother.

Paul, I had no idea. I knew poetry rode in her soul but not that it had once flowed straight onto the page. My mother, a poet!

All week I've been reading and rereading the stack, building a picture of her through bits and pieces of verse. Joy, sunshine, the sea. Love soaring, love vanishing. Love tearing her in two. And I'm starting to understand what she's feeling as she wanders London. For, in her poetry, I see some of those ghosts.

Love,

Margaret

London, England

24 August 1940

Dear Sir or Madam,

Many years ago, a young man named David Graham roomed at this address while a student at the University of Illinois. I know that it has been quite a long time, but I would appreciate any information you could supply.

If you have any information about his whereabouts after leaving Urbana, Illinois, can you please contact me? You can write to me at the Langham Hotel, London. I thank you in advance.

Sincerely,

Mrs. Elspeth Dunn

Chapter Nineteen

~

Elspeth

Place Five
June 30, 1916

Dear Sue,

Sue, YOU'VE DONE NOTHING WRONG. There isn't anything inappropriate in how you're reacting to Iain's death. And how dare anyone try to make you feel otherwise! Cry if you want to. Or sing if you'd rather. Wear the black dress to church, but then change into a bright-yellow one when you're at home. If you want to sit sweating in front of the fire, by all means do so. But then, the next morning, go for a walk barefoot in the coolness of the dew.

Don't for a moment collapse in on yourself. You don't realize what a vibrant force you are on this earth. You are not one meant for mourning. You're meant for living and for loving. As long as you live, you are paying him tribute. As long as you still love him, you are paying him tribute. Keep hold of that, Sue.

And remember, "Here I am." I am just an envelope away.

David

Isle of Skye
7 July 1916

My chevalier,

Even when you don't think you have anything to say, you come up with the perfect words. Of course, I would've been cheered just seeing a grubby envelope addressed in your scrawl, but your words inside act as a balm to my raw heart.

I don't have a yellow dress, but on the way home from the post office I couldn't help but take off my hat and tuck a bunch of blue forget-me-nots in my hair. It was such a beautiful day, warm and drowsy, that it reminded me of my wedding day. Did you know, I would've been married eight years last week? I gathered up some more forget-me-nots, some bright-yellow saxifrage, pansy, red campion, and tied them into a wee posy with the ribbon from my hat. Then I took it to the spot where Iain and I used to play as children and laid it on top of the fairy mound where he gave me my first kiss. I couldn't think of a better place for a memorial to him.

As I stood up there, trying to remember this man I hadn't seen for nearly two years, this husband who suddenly became such a stranger to me, the question of whether or not I still loved him flitted unbidden across my mind.

I think I've always loved Iain in one way or another. I told you I'd known him for years. From childish affection to the "crush" of adolescence. From the blushing love that comes with adulthood to the comfortable love of marriage. So, yes, I still do love him. I suppose I can't imagine *not* loving him, so long have I been doing it.

It's funny you should ask about my poetry. I hadn't written anything for a long time, not since Christmas. I tried to write something last night, as a way to sort out my feelings, but it all sounded so artificial. It didn't flow the way my words did when I was with you. Remember that poem that I wrote in London about you sprawled across the bed with your arm flung over your face? That very movement was a poem in itself. The words were there—I only had to pluck them out of the air and pin them down onto the page. But last night . . . I just couldn't do it. Is my muse gone? Will I not be able to write again?

As strange as this might sound, given the circumstances, I feel better having talked of Iain, almost as if my words here were a eulogy. By talking of him, laying that posy down, I feel as if I'm (gently) closing a door. But when one closes a door, all that remains is to open another one.

Sue

Place Six
July 15, 1916

Sue,

It sounds as if you are doing well. I knew you would figure
out what it was that you needed to do.

We've moved again. I feel like a gypsy, living out of the back
of my flivver, never bedding down in one spot long enough to
wear an indentation into the floor. We're officially *en repos*
again, so we're a good distance behind the lines but still running
the occasional evacuation, usually of the sick (*malades*) rather
than the wounded (*blessés*).

Place Six is one of the most beautiful places I've seen in
France, made even more so by the peacefulness and respite it of-
fers us. I wish I could take your hand and show it to you. We're
staying in a little valley just beyond the town, verdant and dot-
ted with flowers. After smelling powder and blood and the
sickly sweet smell of infection for so long, we can't get enough
of the scent of fresh grass and wildflowers. Here's a poppy for
you, Sue. Press it in your *Huck Finn* and keep it for me.

I remember when you wrote that poem in London. Sue,
could you send that to me? Yeats and Shakespeare are all fine
and good, but I hunger for a bit of original Elspeth Dunn.

Do you notice I'm not worried when you say you'll never
write again? You thought the same right after the war broke out,
and you kept on writing. Darker, more thoughtful stuff, but stuff
all the same. I know you wrote a lot while we were in London.
Your muse hasn't left you, Sue. Be patient.

And you haven't stopped writing, no matter what you say. Your words haven't become artificial. You still write to me, and I don't know that you've ever written more-natural, more-honest thoughts than you write in these letters.

Oh! There's the call for mess. Have to end it for now but wanted to remind you that someone in France is thinking of you.

David

Isle of Skye
22 July 1916

Davey,

Yesterday, I felt rather pensive. As I went about my chores, I couldn't stop thinking about what it means to be married. The expectations the community has of you, the expectations you have of yourself. I'm still not sure what it means to be a widow. I don't know what it is I'm allowed to feel or do.

I'm sure Iain's mother thinks I should spend the rest of my days in mourning, saying a prayer for him each morning, lighting a candle for him each night. As I knelt in the garden, pondering this, I began to think that's what I should be doing.

Then your letter arrived and I was reminded that, of the men in my life who have loved me from far away, here was one who was safe and whole and sound.

I went and dug up that poem to copy over for you. In a rush, those words brought back that lazy afternoon to me. I remember watching you there on the bed, looking so at ease, so happy.

We hadn't eaten, had hardly slept in days, yet you were so perfectly content. Do you remember how you fed me oranges from the fruit bowl with your fingers? I don't know what tasted sweeter—the oranges or you.

The poem reminded me not only of that afternoon but that I've been in love with you for a long time. Rather than spending my time pining away for someone who is never coming back, I could be pining for someone who will. If I say a prayer every morning, Davey, it will be a prayer for you, a prayer that this war ends soon and I have you by my side.

E

Repose

He lies in stillness, bathed in light,
Every muscle touched with gold.
His body draped, his legs outstretched.
The bed caresses, sheets enfold.

He relaxes—open, naked.
Body honest, no dissembling.
Fingers stroke that once were clenching,
Muscles thaw that once were trembling.

His arm is flung across his brow,
His eyes half closed, lashes flutter.
He breathes and sighs, a quiet sound.
Come to me, I hear him mutter.

He stretches, yawning—leonine.
Resettles in his languid pose.
He beckons with one lazy hand
And I join him in his repose.

Place Eight
July 31, 1916

Sue,

We've been jumping around but still *en repos*. We are camped
on the grounds of a marvelous villa, with our tents set up right
in the tree-lined park. There is nothing much to do, except for
the occasional *malade* run, so we've been relaxing, reading,
walking, touring the nearby town. Some days we almost forget
there's a war on.

Your poem brought back memories for me as well. Yes, I remember feeding you those oranges. The juice dribbled out of
the corners of your mouth and I kissed it clean. We took so
many baths! I know, you wished you could've taken that bathtub
home with you as a souvenir. Me, I would've brought those oranges. Or maybe those flowers that you liked so well in Picca-
dilly, the ones you said smelled of the Highlands.

Don't go buying any train tickets yet, but I think that I am
due to go *en permission* at the beginning of September. We're
entitled to *perm* every three months for just a week but can take
a leave of two weeks after nine months. A week isn't nearly long
enough to get from here to Scotland and then back again (which
is why I haven't gone any farther than Paris before now), but

two weeks will give us plenty of time. So be *en garde,* my dear, that if all goes well, I'll be coming to see you in September. Maybe we could meet in Edinburgh?

David

Isle of Skye
7 August 1916

Davey, my Davey!

Dare I even hope that I will see you in September? I know how fickle armies can be when it comes to leave. That's only a month from now—I'll start to dust off my suitcase! Yes, yes, I'll remember to *bring* a suitcase this time. Edinburgh would be lovely. I was quite enamoured of the city. Or we can meet in London again, if that's an easier trip. I don't want to squander a moment of your leave. Someday I will get you up to Skye, but there is time. There is time.

My mother appeared on my doorstep last week with Chrissie and the bairns in tow. With the food shortages in Edinburgh and the Zeppelin attack in the spring, Chrissie thought the children would be much better off up with us on Skye. She and Màthair exchanged a look and Màthair said, "With all your extra space . . . " So here I am, playing "little mother."

Chrissie went back to Edinburgh the very next morning— nurses are in too great a need these days for her to take more than a few days off—but the children settled in quite well. I have only the one bed, and Emily sleeps in here with me. Màthair brought over some tickings, which we stuffed with hay and dried bedstraw. They all seemed to think it a jolly adventure to hike out in search of bedstraw. Emily is the only one who might have a memory of living on Skye. Allie was barely in breeches yet when they left and Robbie was just a wee yin. The boys have really known only city life and view the whole journey to stay with Aunt Elspeth in the Highlands as something akin to Marco Polo's exploration of China.

I know that Màthair and Chrissie mean to distract me, to fill my days and nights so that they aren't so lonely. I can't fault them their thoughtfulness. But they don't know that, ever since the postman brought me a letter from a cheeky American one rainy spring day four and a half years ago, I haven't been lonely anymore. I love you.

E

Place Nine
August 14, 1916

Dear Sue,

When we are all lying about without much to do, we always get into one of two conversations. Well, one of three, I should say. It is unavoidable that the subject of girls comes up at least once in any given conversation. Those who have them will always bring out the creased, folded photos of their girls back home. Pliny, ever the wise guy, brings out a risqué French postcard he bought somewhere and swears quite solemnly that she is his "best gal." The best part? It's a different postcard each time.

The other favorite topic of conversation, unsurprisingly, is

when the war will end. We are always optimistic and usually pin
a vague ending date somewhere around the next major holiday.
At this time of year, we're all cheerfully saying the war will end
by Christmas. Once January rolls around, we'll all be crossing
our fingers for an Easter finale.

The third conversation that always crops up is what we will
be doing after the war. No matter what, this future vision inevi-
tably starts with a feast to rival anything you might find at Delmonico's. Bread with real butter, rich chowders, steaks as
thick as a man's arm, cakes and pies and doughnuts, coffee with
fresh cream, good bourbon. Please excuse the droplets on this
paper; I seem to be drooling.

After our future selves gorge on this much-anticipated feast
(and perhaps work off the meal in a bit of exercise with aforementioned "best gals"), they have to choose a career or path of
life. Good ol' Wart wants nothing more than to settle down with
his girl and start production of Wart Junior. Pliny has grand
plans of running for the U.S. Legislature. He fancies himself a
bigwig, with an endless supply of cigars and women. Gadget—
who is the best of all of us at repairing and generally tinkering
with the flivvers—wants to go work for Henry Ford, designing
cars. Riggles wants to open a showroom and sell them. Harry
will return to his Minna in England and perhaps become a professor. He said he's seen enough maiming and injury here to
turn him off wanting to practice medicine.

Really, though, it's all balloon juice. None of it means anything.
It's fine and good to talk up what you will do when you get out of
this, but the talk is just hot air until you *do* get out of this. We could
talk about our futures today and then lose those futures tomorrow.

Well, except for your Davey. You *do* know I'm coming home to you, don't you, Sue? Made a Faustian bargain to guarantee I would get to see my Sue again. Ah, it's perhaps unpatriotic to talk about *Faust* these days. If any of my buddies were to read this, I'd be tarred and feathered for sure. DAMNED BOCHE RUBBISH! There, maybe they'll focus on the capitalized bit and ignore the rest.

Oh, we're being called to start cranking the Lizzies up. Have to address this and go drop it to be sent.

Kisses!

D

Isle of Skye
22 August 1916

Dear Davey,

What do you tell them about *your* "best girl"? Did you tell them I'm breathtakingly beautiful? Amazingly clever? The most mouthwatering cook this side of Hadrian's Wall?

Oh, Davey! I've just realised that, if all goes well, you'll be eating my world-famous Christmas pudding *in person* this year! You'll be finished with the year you signed on for. See, it doesn't really matter to me if the war ends by Christmas or not, because I, not the Field Service, will have you.

You talked of everyone else and what they hoped for the future, but not a word about yourself. Keeping secrets? "Balloon juice" it may be, but I know you've been thinking of it. You are too much of an optimist, Davey dear, to *not* dream about the future. Will you take me to Delmonico's? Teach me to drive? Whisk me away on ski trips to Michigan? Will we kiss everyone goodbye and sail around the world? Since meeting you, I've done more than I ever thought I would. In the past year alone I've been to London, Paris, and Edinburgh. I've dined at the Carlton, slept at the Langham, and shopped on Charing Cross Road. I feel I could learn to ski or drive a car. With you by my side, I can face any adventure.

> Loving you,
> Sue

Place Ten
August 31, 1916

Sue,

Things are so busy here. I've hardly had a break long enough to change my socks. We serve only a single *poste* here, but so many men move through that *poste* that we have all twenty cars going at any given time. I've just worked nearly forty-eight hours without so much as a catnap. I'm soaking up a heel of bread in lukewarm soup and trying to keep my eyes open long enough to write you back.

God, I'm tired!

No secrets about the future, Sue. I hope to start the very first Highland ballet troupe. And you can be in the barrel of in the and a

Sorry there, dozing . . .

> Kiss you—

Place Ten
September 1, 1916

Sue,

I'm sorry my last letter was so short and so garbled at the
end. I was literally falling asleep over the letter. As my head
bobbed, I swear I saw a prairie dog dash past. I'm sitting in the
ambulance, trying to write this note on my knee while drinking
down a mug (or ten) of coffee.

Still here at————————————and things are as crazy
as can be. No word about the *perm,* but you know I'll let you
know as soon as I hear something.

We've been here—what?—two weeks now, so I don't imagine we can be here too much longer without going *en repos* or
being let *en permission*. If they keep working us at this pace,
we're going to drop. Gadget has come down with something
and is back at the field hospital, so we are short a man.

Let's wait and see about Christmas. You're right, my year is
almost up, but I can reenlist on three-month contracts. Maybe?
The future isn't going anywhere. We'll talk about it when I see
you. Crossing my fingers for that *perm*!

Riggle's cranking her up, so I've got to end for now. Last
swallow of coffee!

    D

Isle of Skye
11 September 1916

Dear Davey,

I hope you've managed a rest. Any word about your leave?
Will you be able to travel up all this way? I can come down
and meet you in London again. I have Màthair on alert—
she'll come over to stay with the children the moment your
telegram arrives.

Lord, but that does sound strange: Màthair will stay with
"the children." They're not mine, but I can't help but feel
some responsibility. After all, I *am* taking part in the shaping
of their young minds!

Chrissie won't recognise her children when she comes
back to pick them up. All are quite brown and freckled from
the sun. The boys have become positively plump on all the
crowdie and cream I've been putting in front of them. Emily
still looks thin to me, but at least she has a bit more energy
now that I've prodded her out into the sunshine.

Please write, no matter how tired you are. Even "I love
you" scrawled on the back of a postcard makes my
heart skip.

And I love *you*.

E

Place Eleven
September 11, 1916

My dear, dear girl,

I'm sorry I haven't written much lately. We were in a really hot zone and were running nearly nonstop. Didn't have time to do much else but drive and keep out of trouble. Even though I didn't have the time or the energy to write to you, Sue, you are never out of my mind.

We're finally *en repos*. I think they could have moved us to the middle of a swamp and we wouldn't have cared, so tired are we. I don't care one way or another where I am, as long as I get to sleep and write to my Sue.

We were quite close to the action and had our fair share of scares in the section. Harry had a shell explode right in front of him while he was driving. He came through with nothing more than a few scratches and ringing ears, but the ambulance was a bit worse for wear in the nose. All of us have found ourselves drowsing at the wheel, but Bucky ended up drifting off the road and smashing into a wall. He's a bit banged up, as you can imagine, and has earned himself a trip out of here.

Not sure how long we'll be *en repos*, but no matter how long it is, it won't seem long enough. I've put a bug in my CO's ear about my *perm*, so we'll wait to see what he says. We've only just gotten to Place Eleven, and I'm sure there are things to get in order before he can sign off on *perms*.

I think I'm going to try to get a nap in before the call for chow. Oh, but it feels so good to stretch out!

Miss you,

D

POSTES ET TÉLÉGRAPHES

PARIS

13 SEP 16

E. DUNN ISLE OF SKYE=

HAVE LEAVE FOURTEEN DAYS WILL WIRE WHEN ARRIVE

IN ENGLAND WILL BE LEAVING IN THE MORNING=

D+

21 Rue Raynouard, Paris, France

September 13, 1916

Sending a postcard in addition to the wire on the chance that you don't get the telegram or that the postcard will beat it there.

I've gotten leave! Fourteen days, if you can believe it. I got my pass to travel to Paris within hours of sending the last letter to you and had my stuff in my bag half a minute after that. Perk of having done so much moving around!

No need for you to come all the way down to London. I'll start heading north, you start heading south, we'll meet somewhere in the middle. . . .

D

POST OFFICE TELEGRAPHS
S 16.04 PORTREE
13 SEP 16

D GRAHAM=
EDINBURGH=
WE WILL MEET IN EDINBURGH=
ST MARYS CATHEDRAL AND THIS TIME I WILL BE THERE=
MY HEART SINGS AGAIN WITH POETRY=
SUE+

Chapter Twenty

~

Margaret

3 September 1940

Dear Maisie,

I never would've guessed that the key to your mother lay in poetry. After meeting her that very first time in the neighbourhood allotment, I would've been tempted to call her one of the earthiest people I know. My gran is a tough old bird, but there was your mother, kicking her shovel and swearing up and down in Gaelic. But, to think, if I didn't take pity on your mother and her poor shovel *and* help her cart those baskets of cabbage home, I might never have met you.

When she pushed open the door to the house and I saw you kicking a jig in the middle of the kitchen in that old sweater and plus fours, I knew that I wanted you for my girl. And, if you wouldn't have me, I'd be your best mate forever and ever if it meant I could be close to you.

Your mam, though, she saw straight to my game. When she was escorting me down the stairs and thanking me, she leaned in and said, "She thinks with her heart. Don't shatter it." That's why it took me two weeks to come calling again.

But to think she wrote love poetry! I suppose that's why she saw right through me the moment I clapped eyes on you.

Really, you've never seen her write a word of poetry? After your letter, I looked into her, and she has seven books to her name. Seven! My gran has been around for twice as long, and she couldn't put together a decent stanza if the fate of the world depended on it.

What have you discovered? I don't suppose you've come across a poem with the name and address of "Davey"?

Love,
Paul

Beagan Mhìltean, Skye
6 September 1940 (What day is it, even?)

Dear Paul,

No, no addresses between the pages, but I did find flowers, blades of grass, curls of wool, sprinkles of sand. It looked as though she carried the books across the island, catching whatever she came across within the pages.

Out of Chaos, her last book, with the red cover barely creased, had pictures tucked throughout. A cheerful young man in a checked jacket grins from one. In another, a dark-haired

woman in a pale flimsy dress sits in a garden of flowers, gazing
wistfully at the camera. The same man, now in a robe and mortarboard, stands next to a tiny sapling in yet another, his chin
jutting out proudly.

The last picture, hidden all the way in the back, shows a couple on a street, the pedestrians and vehicles a blur behind them.
The man has both hands wrapped around the woman's waist
and leans in to whisper something in her ear. The woman holds
one hand to the side of her face, as though trying to hide from
the camera, but instead laughs with head thrown back. In pen,
across the corner of the photograph, someone wrote "1915.
Us." Although the picture is grainy, the man is as in the other
two photos. He's the same as the ambulance driver painted
across the back of Seo a-nis. The woman is my mother.

The photo is so nonchalant, so un-self-conscious. Just the
two of them, caught in an unlikely photograph, a moment of
transition in a secret affair. Cautiousness in the fingers curved
against her cheek giving way to utter abandon in that laugh. In
that instant, the blur of the city behind them doesn't matter.
This must be the London my mother is looking to find, the London she wishes she could capture again. An instant of aloneness
while the war rushes on around them.

He's her muse, I know it. Although the name "David" never
appears in any of her books, I know the poems are for him. The
person she writes to, she calls "my magnet," "my warm summer
night," and the one "my heart flies towards." Gran won't say a
word. She just nods and taps the stack of poetry books, as
though they hold all the secrets of the universe.

And maybe they do. In school, I couldn't find a theme in a poem if my soul depended on it. What makes me think I can find a life in a poem now?

There was one that Mother used to recite to me at bedtime, between the fairy stories and Gaelic lullabies, a poem about the wind coming off the sea, crisp and salt-tanged. Roaring across the water and straight up the crags, hurtling fingers of cold against anyone who stood in the way. I'm not sure if it was her own poetry, as I haven't found it in any of her books, but it's the only one she ever taught me.

Walking the island here, I remembered that poem. I stand up on the hills, looking out over the sea, and shout all of the lines into the wind. It whips my dress through my legs, sprays my bare arms, puts the taste of salt on my lips. And I know what that poem means.

Because, as much as the wind batters you up on the hills, as much as it demands to be noticed, the moment you climb back down, it begins to fade. And it's no less intense down below, to be sure. The gulls fight it; the grasses blow flat. It's there, but, after a while, it drifts from your mind. It's a given, a constant, an expectation. You don't think about it being there until one day, suddenly, it rushes right over you, fills your mouth and your ears and your soul and you remember what it's like to breathe. You've been breathing every day but, in that instant, feel completely alive.

From the day you came into my kitchen with that basket of cabbages, you've been there. Always with me, like the wind. But that first time I found a letter from you in the post, my heart leapt as it never had before. You rushed right over me and I knew I was in love.

I wish you were here with me to feel the wind. It's poetry in itself.

Love,
Maisie

London, England
28 August 1940

Dear Sir or Madam,

Many years ago, a young man named David Graham was a student at the University of Illinois. He graduated in 1913, with a degree in natural sciences. I don't know if he is active in the University of Illinois Alumni Association, but I understand that you often hear news from alumni and maintain a record of their whereabouts since leaving the university.

If you have any information on David Graham, can you please contact me? You can write to me at the Langham Hotel, London. I thank you in advance.

Sincerely,
Mrs. Elspeth Dunn

Chapter Twenty-one

~

Elspeth

Somewhere between Edinburgh and London
September 22, 1916

Oh, Sue!

It was so hard to get back on the train this time. Not that parting was ever easy before, but it is especially hard now that I know what it is to be separated from you. The last time we parted and I got on that train, heading for a boat to take me across the channel, my mind was so full of you but at the same time so full of anticipation and uncertainty. This time, I am sitting and gazing out at the English countryside blurring by the window and all I can think about is that every hedgerow and neat green field we pass is one more hedgerow and green field between us.

I'm going to mail this before leaving England, so I can write a bit more freely than I can under the watchful eyes of the censors. I couldn't tell you face-to-face, but I'm becoming a bit tired of it all. The last *poste* we were at, out of Château Billemont, was so utterly consuming and utterly exhausting, but at least I felt like I was involved in the war, more so than I have at some of the other *postes*. We always seem to be either on the move or *en repos*.

We hear the shells, sometimes see them when they fall on the roads, but that's as close as we get to the action. We live vicariously through the stories we hear from the *blessés*. Sometimes I feel as if we're hanging around outside the cinema, trying to piece together the flicker from the bits and pieces we overhear as the patrons come out of the theater.

That time I ran up the ridge to help that wounded *brancardier*, in full view of the Boches and their guns, the familiar prickles of danger and excitement grabbed me. I felt so alive. It was as if I were scrambling up the wall with those squirrels again. To be *doing* something instead of just waiting back and watching others do it. I tell you, it was so hard to go back to my usual work after getting out of the hospital.

Do you understand why I couldn't tell this all to you, Sue? You would've wrapped those surprisingly strong arms of yours around me and not let go. Not that I would've minded too terribly being held captive by such a jailer, but, like I told you, I need to finish out my year. I have to accomplish something in my life. If I can't stick it out for a whole year, then what can I stick out? You don't want a man who can't finish anything.

Speaking of the future, I can't believe you got an apartment in Edinburgh! Only for the week, but still. You knew what it would mean to me. For a guy who's been living out of an ambulance, to walk up and see those curtains at the windows, it was just like coming home.

I'm still tired, but I'd much rather be tired from an excess of lovemaking than from an excess of work. I didn't want to waste a moment of my time with you on sleeping. That's what the train journey back to London is for.

Despite my tiredness, I do feel like a new man. Clean, well fed, clothes washed and mended, warm new greatcoat. Body and spirit sated. You laughed at me, but I had to save up my "satiations"! I've gone so long without that I wanted to put in extra stock, the memories to be pulled out and savored as needed.

Even that one incident couldn't spoil things for me. I know you were upset, Sue, but you did nothing wrong. He shouldn't have said the things he did, but I'm sure he didn't mean anything by them. I hope you've gotten past it.

On that note, I think I'll end for now so I can close my eyes and pull out one of those aforementioned memories. What do you think—the one in the bathtub?

David

Somewhere between Edinburgh and Skye
22 September 1916

Davey,

I hate this! I hate having nothing but these snatched days with you! It is so hard to lose myself completely in them, because I can hear the ticktock down to your departure, like that blasted alarm clock in our Paris hotel.

And to have part of our precious holiday ruined by my brother. Oh, he makes me furious! He's not been right since his discharge anyhow, but then add his problems with Kate and with Iain's death. None of it is my fault, yet he heaped it all on me. I'm telling myself that he didn't mean what he said, that they were words spoken only in anger, that I'll get home and we'll go walking on the shingle together to look for stones, the way we always did. But the way he spat at my feet, as if I were nothing, the way he looked when he walked away. I fear something broke in that instant, and I have no idea how to hold it together.

Not that I'm very good at mending broken things. But you, at least, I can do something about.

Davey, if only you knew what good you were doing, even far back from the front lines. How you've sacrificed so much time with me just to be there. If you knew the importance of your work, the way that you *matter*, you wouldn't worry that you should be doing more. You wouldn't envy those in No Man's Land.

You don't know how glad I am that you are far from the danger. You don't know how glad I am to keep you safe and whole for another trip to Edinburgh. That first night, after you arrived, I lay awake next to you for the longest time, just watching. Your eyelashes fluttering, your inhales and exhales. I rested my fingers right on your bare chest, simply to feel your heartbeat and know that you were *there*. And, Davey, how I thanked God right then and there for bringing you back to me. I couldn't bear to lose you too.

I could already see these doubts in you, in the way you

brushed off what was going on in your section, in the way you
shrugged when I said how lucky we were to be here together.
And that's why Finlay made me so angry, to stir up your doubts
that way, to make you feel you were doing wrong by being here,
with me.

Because, Davey, there's no more important place for you to
be. You're my breath, my light, the one my heart flies towards.
You said you worried you'd take away from what I had with
Iain. That you didn't want to compete with a memory. That you
didn't want to be less of a man than he was. But, Davey, he's
gone. And I'm not back in my cottage, missing him. All week
I've been right there. With you.

    Sue

21 Rue Raynouard, Paris, France
September 25, 1916

Sue,

Got back here to Paris and who do you suppose I found?
Pliny, Harry, Riggles, Wart, and a few more of the guys all
camped out at the headquarters here at Rue Raynouard. They
came up the line only yesterday.

Just when I thought things were getting to be boring around
here, opportunity presents itself. The French have asked for a
section to go up to————near————. From what they
tell us, it has been a bit of a hike for the *brancardiers* to maneuver
the *blessés* by hand back to the *poste de secour*. Since the Boches
took the nearby hill, the road to the *poste* is exposed and under

fire. They want a fleet of fast ambulances to speed almost right up to the line and back. This route will go closer to the front-line trenches than any of the other routes. And it will have to be done at night.

Instead of sending Section One up there, they created a whole new section, with good ol' Pliny promoted to command. They're sending him some new recruits to fill the ranks, but Pliny is quite obstinate in insisting on the fastest, most fool-hardy veterans he can find. They gave him leave to pick a hand-ful of guys from Section One, and the rest will be assigned either from the other sections or from new recruits coming in. We've all heard stories and know what a tough sector it will be to work. You have to be fast and nimble.

Since yours truly is both fast and nimble (and, I suppose, foolhardy), Pliny asked me to transfer over to his section. Can you believe it, Sue? Not only does it sound like just the ticket for what's been ailing me, but Harry and all of my old pals will be there. I think it will be bully!

The French must be planning a big push, as they want ambu-lances in place by a week from last year. We're waiting for the rest of the section to arrive and for our brand-new Lizzies to be delivered. For now we're resting up.

More later!

David

21 Rue Raynouard, Paris, France
September 27, 1916

Dear Sue,

Just got your letter here, the one you wrote on the train. Don't worry about your brother—it's not like I haven't had a shiner before. He was only being protective. You are his only sister, after all. I understand. What brother wouldn't fly off the handle to see his sister with an American? You forget, we're all outlaws and cowboys. I hope you got things sorted with him when you got back up to Skye. And you will. Siblings cannot stay angry forever. Especially not Finlay and you.

And, Sue, though I was disillusioned, trust that it wasn't with you. Never in a million years. True, I was fed up with the Field Service and my inactivity behind the lines. And, true, things felt different on this trip, what with Iain being gone and all. So many of your recent letters have been about him. Understandably so. But it's funny, isn't it, that on this trip I felt him more between us than before.

Believe me, those disillusions vanished the moment I lay my head on your lap. I told you that seeing your name outside the apartment felt like coming home. And, Sue, that's enough for me. To know that I'm doing something worthwhile here and that you're waiting for me in Scotland. That's all I need.

Well, after all of that worry about the new recruits, we've been sent the best of the bunch. Among others, we have Rex Redman, the stunt cyclist. Leo Nickles, a crackerjack pilot who was with the Escadrille. My personal favorite, Roy Jansson,

race-car driver. I actually saw him race at Speedway Park in
Chicago. Can you believe he got up to a speed of 100 miles per
hour?

The men from the other sections have begun to trickle in.
Anyone who has made a name for himself in his section has
been recommended for what is already unofficially known as
"Plinston's Boys." They've promised us one hot sector after another.

We should be moving out of here tomorrow or the next day,
so I'm not sure when I'll be able to write again. Harry has a
stack of letters for Minna, and I'll try to slip my own envelope
on the bottom of the stack.

    David

October 4, 1916

Oh, Sue,

This is what I was born to do! You can't imagine the exhila-
ration. Yes, I'm working harder than I've ever worked before
and I am dog-tired at the end of the day, and, yes, I realize that
my job is just duck soup compared to what those boys out in No
Man's Land are working at, but this is what I needed.

We work runs to only two *poste de secours,* both accessible by
a single road, a road as straight as a yardstick and nearly as narrow. We have hardly any cover, and the Boches have recently
taken a position that gives them a perfect shot of anyone who
happens to be caught on that road. The stretchers used to be

taken back along this road by hand, but the Boches had to pick off a fair number of *brancardiers* before the French finally got the message.

When we get a call and start heading for the *postes*, a certain spot by a derelict barn marks the unofficial boundary between the shelled zone and the safe. As we approach that barn, there's an instant where we toss any fears out the window and open the flivver up as much as she will go.

We can't think as we drive down this Corridor of Death, we can't concentrate, we can't reason. We just look at the brown ridge of the rear trench that marks the end of the corridor and forget all else. It takes only twenty-six seconds to drive this road, but it feels like twenty-six minutes, so we've taken to counting it aloud. Yesterday I made it in twenty-five.

Oh, God, I don't know how Riggles could be content with selling autos after this is all over with. I don't know how Harry can be content teaching whining undergraduates. I don't know how any of us can be content with doing anything that doesn't make us feel invincible.

David

Isle of Skye
4 October 1916

Davey,
My brother is gone.
When he walked away from me in Edinburgh, he walked

away from the whole family. He didn't even send Màthair a tele-gram to say goodbye. She hasn't come out of her bed in days.

The way he's always kept an eye on the horizon, I think we all half-expected this would come, especially after his discharge. Deep in my heart, I've always thought he'd leave one day. Màthair said he only ever stayed on Skye because of me, that when he saw, growing up, that I would never set foot on that ferry, he tucked away his wishes and let Da take him out on the fishing boat. If I couldn't leave, he wouldn't either.

But now he did! Without a backwards glance, he sailed away. I should be glad he escaped the fishing and crofting life he never looked for, but I can't help but cry. After all this time, he did it without me. Worse, he did it to spite me.

I wrote Finlay a letter, even though I have nowhere to send it. I told him I was sorry but that he was wrong, that "my American," as he put it, had made me a promise. My American isn't going to forget about me up here on my island. He isn't going to sail back to America without a backwards glance. "Here I am," he said to me once. And he is. He's there, no matter what happens. And, in another month, his contract will be finished, and he'll come up here and sweep me away.

You promised me Christmas, Davey. I know you won't walk away like my brother. Please.

Sue

France
October 18, 1916

Sue,

I hate having to say this, but I don't know if I'll be home by Christmas. I know you've probably thrown this letter across the room already, but once you pick it back up, hear me out.

I wasn't happy back when I told you I would renew only until December. The glamor of this all, the excitement I'd felt last fall when I volunteered, had started to fade. I wasn't doing much but sitting around behind the lines waiting for the next sector. I wanted nothing more than to go on permanent *repos* with you.

But now, with the new section, I feel so alive. You wouldn't believe how much. Sue, for the first time, I matter.

Remember, I couldn't cut it as a student. I couldn't cut it as a teacher. Hell, I couldn't even cut it as a son. My dad still thinks I'm a disappointment. But now, using the bravado that did nothing but get me in trouble as a kid, I'm succeeding. Guys who otherwise wouldn't make it now do. And all in the back of my flivver. Mine.

So, you see, I can't leave now. Not when I've really begun. Can't you see that, Sue? Would you pull me away from all this just when I'm needed most?

David

Isle of Skye
1 November 1916

"Would you pull me away from all this just when I'm needed most?" Yes, yes, I would, especially when you're needed even more here. Davey, I'm pregnant. So stop all of this nonsense and come home.

France
November 12, 1916

This is how you tell a fellow news like this? This wasn't supposed to happen. That's why I brought the French letters. We're not in a position to make a decision like this. A family, Sue? You're still mourning, I'm still "playing war." We're seven hundred miles apart. And look at how your brother acted in Edinburgh. I deserved each blow. After all, I'm the American who came between you and your husband. I'm the one who caused the rift with your brother. Why would your family welcome me after that?

Isle of Skye
29 November 1916

Then come and take me away from here! Whisk me away to America, where there is no war or disapproving brothers. The neighbours are already starting to whisper and, oh Davey, I just want to go away with you and start on that future we keep talking about.

Yes, this is enormous. It's overwhelming. It's even a bit scary. But how can the thought of impending fatherhood be scarier than speeding down the "Corridor of Death" every day?

It terrifies me too. The way I've already torn my own family in two, I'm not fit to raise a child. Maybe I was right all those years ago when I said I shouldn't be a mother. I don't think I can do this.

Davey, I need you to be the strong one. I need you to be brave for the both of us. Please come here and take me away. I feel invincible when I'm with you.

I'm tired now. I don't want to argue about this. It's a fact and not worth fighting about. Amidst all this war, all this death, we've made life. The baby, it's just another adventure. And, remember, I can face any adventure with you by my side.

Sue

December 3, 1916

Dear Elspeth,

I wish I weren't writing you. Months ago, Dave gave me this envelope and told me to mail it if something ever happened.

We were doing a run four nights ago. When we got there, we found that the dugout had just been hit. Doctors, orderlies, *blessés*—gone. An officer was trying to put some sort of order on the situation, directing those coming up from the first-line trench.

Having a little medical training, I started checking over the *blessés* coming in, deciding who was going to even make it back to the *poste de triage*. Those *brancardiers* still upright were dumping their loads and heading back out as fast as they could stumble. Dave, fool that he is, jumped into the trench and followed after. He came back a few times, ignored my shouts, and went back out. One time he didn't come back.

He had no business being up over the first line, but you know Dave. He never would listen to prudence. He did what had to be done, though.

I debated for those four days whether or not to mail you this letter. I kept hoping he'd come limping out of No Man's Land with an amusing story about yet another lucky escape. It wasn't to be.

There's not much I can do for you from here, but please write to Minna if there's anything you need. I know about your situation. Dave told me that night, as we were speeding along to the *poste*. Yes, he was shocked and scared. But that night he was hopeful. And quite happy.

So to satisfy the last wish of the best friend I could ever hope to have . . .

Harry Vance

Sue, my own sweet girl.

This is the letter you were never supposed to read. If you are, it means this is the last one I'll ever send.

As I'm writing this, it's May and I've just gotten back from seeing you in Paris. Your stack of increasingly fran-

tic letters waited for me upon my return. As I read them,
I began to realize exactly how scared and worried you
must have been, so far away from everything happening
here. I don't want you to have to go through that again,
not knowing, so I'm doing what works best for us. I'm
writing you a letter.

I don't know when you'll read this. It could be next
month, it could be six months from now, it could be a
year. I hope it's never. I don't know what the world will
be like then. I don't know what sort of things we'll have
been writing about. I don't know if you'll have found
yourself another handsome American ambulance driver.

I can say with certainty (even looking into the future)
that I haven't and never will find another Sue. You are the
reason I frown at the sunrise and smile at the sunset.
Frown because I have to face the day alone, without you
by my side. Smile because that's one less day we have to
spend apart.

You wrote in one of your letters that you didn't think
you were strong enough. You said, "I can't do it all on my
own without knowing you exist in this world." You *are*
strong, Sue. Look at you—you crossed the English
Channel for me! When I see the things you did for me, it
makes me wish I was a stronger man for you.

I know you wish I had never gotten involved with this
war over here, that when I got to London I had just
stayed on that train and raced clear up to Skye, never
leaving again. But I had to do this. I couldn't come to you
as a failure, Sue. I had to prove I was *something*. You al-

ways call me a boy. I needed to grow up and become a man.

I know you, my dear. I know that right now you are shaking your head angrily at my words and saying, "But you *didn't* fail. You got me to fall in love with you! *I'm* your success." You are my success, Sue. And I know that. I don't know what I did right in my life, but it must've been something pretty worthy for me to have gotten you. My pearl.

I regret not telling you this. I want to be the first thing your bleary eyes focus on in the morning. I want to watch you wash your face and slide on your stockings. I want to cook you breakfast and kiss the egg from the corner of your mouth. I want to curl up by the window, you tucked on my lap, reading, writing, talking, breathing. I want to warm up your bare feet between my knees in bed. I want to fall asleep with your hair tickling my chin.

I would have moved to Skye and suffered through the disapproval of your neighbors and your family, if that was what you wanted. I would have gone to the farthest reaches of Siberia, if that was what you wanted. I know that now I'm in a place neither of us would have chosen.

You said once a long while ago that it was too clichéd to say you could love someone forever. Is there a word that means "longer than forever"? That will be how long I love you.

Now, forever, and beyond that. I love you.

David

Chapter Twenty-two

~

Margaret

Glasgow
6 September

Margaret,

It's weighed on me for years that I was the cause of my sister's sadness. I'm sure she blames me still.

You see, I had a girl named Kate. When I went off to soldier, she wove a lock of her hair into a rosette and stitched it to my shirt, near my heart, so that she'd always be with me.

Then came Festubert and I returned home a leg short, wanting nothing more than to bury my face on her shoulder. But that first moment, when I tried to draw her into my arms, she flinched. Literally flinched. She slowly stopped coming around, but, really, that made it easier. If she wasn't there, I wouldn't have to see her eyes sneak to my folded trouser leg, wouldn't

have to feel the air between us as she stepped aside to let me
pass.

I thought I understood. What lass wants a cripple for a husband? Even when I received my prosthetic, I knew it wouldn't
matter. She already felt so far away.

Then Willie came home on leave. I was out at Elspeth's new
cottage, carving a mantelpiece. Willie found me sitting behind
the kailyard with a lapful of wood shavings, and he tossed off his
tunic to help. There, sewn to his shirt, right over his heart, was a
golden rosette of hair.

We scuffled. He kept saying that we can't help who we love.
I think I broke his nose. Màthair was furious, and Elspeth cried
and cried. Willie left the next day and didn't come home on
leave again.

And I thought that was that. I simmered, but Willie left and I
could carve Elspeth's mantel and try to forget I'd ever met Kate.
But peace doesn't last long. Elspeth received a letter from the
War Office. Iain had been officially declared dead.

Those months passed in a blur. Iain, closer to me than my
own brother, was gone. We'd set off for France with a lot of
bravado and a promise to watch out for one another. I'd failed.
Those were black days, to be sure. Elspeth was better off than I
was. Alasdair's bairns had come to stay with her, to fill her days.
Since Kate left me, I had no one. I spent my time alone, walking
the hills with my cane and a flask. When I went to Edinburgh
for a check on my prosthetic, the doctor took me to task for
abusing it so on the climbs. I didn't care. I needed the pain.

But on my way back to Waverley Station, I saw Elspeth. She

wasn't back on Skye, mourning Iain. She was in an embrace right there on the street, with a stranger.

I know I wasn't being fair when I squared her around and gave her a piece of my mind. The man pushed between us, as if it were any business of his. He wasn't even from here; he was just an American. How could she forget about Iain like that? Only months after his death, and here she was throwing herself at someone else. How could she betray him, and with an American?

She stood with head down and let me say my piece. Whispered that she hadn't forgotten Iain and never would. But then she started to cry, and the American stepped between us again. I went for him, asked what he was doing going after other men's wives while soldiers were dying in the trenches. And Elspeth's eyes flared up.

Yes, men were dying in the trenches. But, back at home, people were living. *She* was living. And I was never to step between her and her life again. She threw back her shoulders in that stubborn way I knew so well and said that we can't help who we love. Just as Willie had.

Hearts meant more than blood? Now I knew why Willie thought that. But he was only a lad. Elspeth was supposed to be the smart one. The loyal one. The one who'd never turn away from her family or the promises she made. It was always supposed to be Elspeth, Iain, and me against the world. I told her to choose. Chin lifted, she took the American's arm. I spat, said she was a fool, said that my whole family were fools. One day he'd play her false, but I wouldn't stay to pick up the pieces. And I didn't.

I did write to Màthair once, a few weeks later. I asked if Elspeth had listened to what I said. I asked if she was still with the
American. Màthair wrote back that I should know well enough
when to quit, that Elspeth didn't much care what anyone said
these days. She'd just received word that her American had
died, and it took all of Màthair's strength to keep Elspeth from
following after.

Of course, I felt rotten after that. Who wouldn't? But I was
young and stupid and thought that any apology was too late.
The past is past, Màthair always said, and so I stepped away
from it all. If Elspeth decided to forgive me one day, she'd find
me. At least that's what I thought at the time. And, lad that I
was, it made sense.

Now I know it was stubbornness—foolish stubbornness—
and I'm too old to keep waiting for forgiveness. For breaking
her heart, for breaking our family, the forgiveness might never
come.

I'm asking for it now. I know how things can change in an instant in wartime. I know how quickly things can be lost. If you
hear from your mother again, please tell me. I need to write to
her. After all this time, I need to tell her that I'm sorry.

Love,
Uncle Finlay

London, England
2 September 1940

Dear Sir,

Many years ago, a young man named David Graham volunteered with the American Field Service, near the beginning of the Great War. I understand the American Field Service Association plans reunions of the ambulance sections and maintains a publication with news and information about the former members.

If you have any information on David Graham, no matter how slim, can you please contact me? You can write to me at the Langham Hotel, London. I thank you in advance.

Sincerely,
Mrs. Elspeth Dunn

Chapter Twenty-three

⌒

Elspeth

Kriegsgefangenen-Sendung, Postkarte
January 2, 1917

Sue,

If you get a letter from Harry, *do not open it*! Throw it away. Never read it.

I know you must've been worried, not hearing from me for a while, but trust me when I say I couldn't write to you before now.

I am fine, but I've been taken prisoner. I'm not sure how much I'm allowed to write or how often I'll be allowed to send letters, but you can write to me at the address on the other side of this card.

Can you please write to Harry to let him know what happened and give him this address?

I'm sorry I wasn't there for Christmas with you, but, as you can see, I didn't break my promise to you. I just need to delay its fulfillment.

I love you. More than you could ever know.

David

Isle of Skye
22 January 1917

Davey,

I can hardly write through the tears. Your postcard—precious bit of cardboard!—is crushed in my fist, and I'm writing you with my other hand. Màthair tried to pry it from my hand to read, but I wouldn't let it go. She saw your handwriting and then ushered everyone out of the room.

I knew you couldn't be dead. I suppose everyone says that about those they love. But I still felt you! As long as my heart was whole and beating, I knew you must still exist on this earth.

And you do! Every day that I thought about you and wept over you, you were thinking about me with just as much force.

Oh, my darling, my love. My own amazing boy. Me—the poet—lost for words.

Your Sue

Isle of Skye
24 January 1917

Davey,

I've found them. My words, that is.

How are you? Really? Do you need anything? Are you warm enough?

I can't bear the thought of you in a prison. It must be awfully cold and uncomfortable, if it's anything like in the books. Can I send you packages?

It has been a bleak few months, for a lot of reasons, but now I see a ray of sunshine through the clouds. I can crumple up the poems I've been writing since December and toss them in the flames.

This is the slow time of the year. Much sitting in front of the fire, reading and writing. I've been trying to get the children interested in poetry, but, alas, no such luck. Are you allowed to have your books there?

As much as the thought of you in prison makes me shiver, I can't help but be glad that you're alive, that, God willing, you'll be back in my arms before long.

    Yours,

    Sue

February 7, 1917

Sue,

I'm allowed to send only two letters a month (not to exceed six pages) and four postcards. I really should send the occasional letter and postcard to my mother, Evie, and Harry, so you won't be able to get nearly the bounty of letters you did before. The bounty of thoughts, however, will remain undiminished.

As far as I know, you are able to send as many packages and letters as you wish. If you can, there are many things I need. I didn't have my bag with me when I was taken, so I can use a lot of basic things: comb, toothbrush, soap, spare socks and shirt. I've been borrowing these from some of the others. Would it be possible for you to send a blanket? And books! Any and all reading material you can get your hands on. I've been reading and rereading your two precious letters (the rest back in my duffel bag—I should write to Harry about that). All I had on me when I went over was your picture and "Repose" tucked into my jacket pocket, but I could live on nothing but sand and water for years as long as I had those two things.

What I wouldn't give for things to be back to the way they were in Edinburgh. Just you, me, and a quiet place. Just you and me.

I love you,
Davey

P.S. How have you been feeling? You haven't mentioned anything about the baby.

Isle of Skye
28 February 1917

I wanted to send the package as soon as possible, so I hope I've found everything you need—some more socks (I had a whole basket knit for you, so you will have no shortage of socks, my love!); the only men's shirts I could find in Portree; comb, tooth-brush, and tooth powder; soap; a package of handkerchiefs. Wondered if you needed shaving tackle but didn't know if you'd be allowed to receive that. The blanket is the one from my own bed.

Harry's already taken care of your kit bag. When he thought you weren't coming back, he packed up the contents and sent them to your mother. He kept aside your copy of *Huck Finn* and your Bible, which he sent to me. He's no fool; he knew what I would want most of all to remember you by. I know you have a greater need for Huckleberry's companionship than I do. Anyway, I have my own copy. I return him to you.

I rummaged quickly through my own stock and tossed in some Byron and Plutarch, supplemented with a few penny dreadfuls I found in town. I'm sorry I couldn't fit any more in this package. The blanket took up nearly all of the room. I have some fresh notepaper for you tucked inside Byron and a couple of pencils.

I want to hold on to the Bible for now, if you don't mind. Consider it your pair of socks.

I never stop thinking about you and wishing you were here.

Love,

Sue

P.S. I'm not pregnant any longer. Maybe it is for the best.

March 16, 1917

My dear Sue,

Many thanks for the parcel. Everything is much appreciated, especially the socks.

I'm quite comfortable here. The sole drawback I see is that I'm the only American in this camp. There isn't even an Englishman to converse with. French and Russians and Poles. A few of the Frenchmen have a bit of English, and I am starting to learn a few words of Russian, but it's not the same.

Speaking of which, the books are perfect, Sue. Don't you worry. Even the "penny dreadfuls." The lack of a library was making me crazy. Those of us here who are of a literary bent devour (and then re-devour) anything with words. I've been borrowing whatever I can in French. Anytime you have a bit of space in a package, my dear girl, please slip in a couple of volumes for me. Anything and everything is welcome. What I wouldn't do for a *Trib*! Again, another "alas!"

Thinking of you,

David

P.S. Maybe it is for the best. Everything is so uncertain now. A guy in prison isn't exactly father material. We can talk about it properly when I get home. I love you.

Chapter Twenty-four

~

Margaret

London
7 September 1940

Oh, Màthair,

I don't know what else to do. I've been in London these past
two months with a suitcase of letters, reading and rereading
Davey's scrawl. I've written to every address I can think of—
his parents' house in Chicago, the apartment he shared with
Harry, his rooming house, his sister's house, even his university
alumni organization, and the American Field Service
Association—any address I could find that could lead to someone, anyone, who might know what happened to him. To "my
American."

And I haven't received a single response. I know, after
decades, I shouldn't expect any. People move on, lives continue. I shouldn't expect that these people still live at the same

addresses. I shouldn't expect that they know anything about Davey. I shouldn't expect that they can bandage up my heart.

I've spent these long weeks of waiting just wandering around London. Going to every place we walked together, every railing he brushed against, every bend in the road where he stopped to touch my face. Did I ever tell you about the Christmas I spent with Chrissie in Edinburgh, when Davey and I both went outside at midnight just to feel the other across the miles? I thought if I went to all the right spots in London, I could feel him: his breath on my face, his voice in my ear, his hand in mine. I thought that I could find those moments and catch them up in my fingers.

But this isn't the London where I gave away my heart. This is a city prepared for siege. Everything's a little dimmer, a little greyer. Shop windows we pressed against are full of tinned food and gas masks. Doorways we paused in to kiss are edged in sandbags. There's no romance beneath the chandeliers of the Langham. These days, it's crowded with uniforms and officiousness. The war is everywhere.

There was one moment when I stepped out of the hotel and swore I saw him on the other side of the street, standing on the steps of All Souls Church. But a bus passed and the image was gone. Even here, nothing but ghosts.

Màthair, there's no hint of Davey here. Not any longer. Not even in our old room at the Langham. I thought being where we once were, would draw him to me. That I'd send out these letters and finally get some answers. That I'd finally find out what happened to my American.

I'm tired. Half my life has been waiting, it feels, and I don't know how much longer I can do it. It's exhausting.

I'll stay another week at the Langham, just to be sure no letters come, but then I'll head back towards Edinburgh, head back to again wall up my memories and continue waiting. I know no other way to be. I miss my Margaret so.

> Love,
> Elspeth

9 September 1940

Maisie,

Have you heard from your mother? Please tell me you have. Is she well?

The moment I heard the news about the bombs in London, I hoped she was already out of the city. None of the reports I've read seem to know exactly how many planes there were, exactly how many buildings were hit. Hundreds? Thousands? But London is still burning, they say. They are calling it a blitz.

I'll find out more but, please, tell me your mother got out in time.

> Love,
> Paul

Beagan Mhìltean, Skye
Saturday, 14 September 1940

Paul,

Mother sent a letter that arrived at the same time as yours, only hers was written two days before.

Oh, Paul, we had no idea! We'd had no mail, much less a newspaper, for days. A blitz attack that left all of London burning? Gran sent me straight into Portree for news and for a telegram to Emily, in case Mother had left London earlier and made it to Edinburgh.

I can scarcely believe what I'm reading, Paul. Hundreds of bombs, all over the city. Sure, there have been air raids in London before. We've all had air raids. But for so much so fast on one city . . . I just can't comprehend. When they fall, they don't discriminate. The London my mother knew truly is gone.

And then almost every day since! A city besieged. I hope, I pray, she's not there, but Emily said the house in Edinburgh is still shut tight, so I do what she's been doing all these months. I wait. And watch the post.

I know that you're out there flying in it all. Paul, please be safe. For me.

Love,
Maisie

LONDON STANDS STRONG AFTER
10TH NIGHT OF ATTACKS
London, Tuesday, 17 September

After hundreds of German raiders swarmed over London last night and early this morning in the fiercest air attack yet, the city stands strong, with only a single casualty and minimal damage.

During the day, London heard a number of alarms, including one lasting nearly four hours—the longest yet for a daytime warning. The attack was made difficult by patches of fog hanging low over the city. The sirens began again in earnest sometime after 8 P.M., when the skies cleared, and they continued, unabated, until 2:42 A.M., when the anti-aircraft shells finally succeeded in driving off the Nazi attackers. But the citizens of London did not rest for long in their shelters, as a new warning sounded at 3:52 A.M. and another wave of raiders hit the besieged city.

High-explosive bombs were dropped in Central London in wave after wave, damaging buildings and shattering windows within a half-mile radius. Incendiary bombs fell on a popular shopping area and a number of residential neighbourhoods, keeping the fire watches busy with their gallant fight. In Portland Place, a heavy bomb fell, destroying a coal-gas main in the street and causing damage to the fashionable Langham Hotel. . . .

Chapter Twenty-five

~

Elspeth

Isle of Skye
6 April 1917

My love,

I'm not sure if I can send food as well, but I can't bear to think of you hungry when I have so much more. Apples, bread, smoked sausage, cheese, beans, rice, salted herring, onions, jam. Not much fresh coming through my little garden yet, so I've included some dried peas. I hope they all make it to you with no trouble.

This time last year you were in hospital and I was frantic with worry. I won't say I don't worry about you now, as I worry every day we're apart, but at least I know that you are safe and whole and missing me dearly.

I've also started writing to Minna. Did you know she's had a baby? The bonniest wee boy, with a sprinkling of pale hair, like

Harry. She sent a photo. Do you hear from Harry at all? It must be hard for her to be alone.

I'm tucking a kiss inside this envelope with the letter. Be sure that you grab tight to it before it wiggles out and escapes!

Love,

Sue

Kriegsgefangenen-Sendung, Postkarte
April 23, 1917

Sue,

Last night I saw the most beautiful sunset. It made me think about the time we took the tram out to Portobello and watched the sunset from the beach. Even though the water was freezing, you dared me to roll up my trousers and wade in. Then you sat on my lap and buried your toes in the sand and we shared that god-awful pie that you made. God-awful or not, I wish I had that pie now. And the sand. And the sunset. But, most of all, I wish I had you.

Davey

Isle of Skye
2 May 1917

Davey,

Of course I remember that sunset. I think that was the first time I'd ever sat and just watched the sun slip below the horizon.

I truly felt the earth rotating beneath me. Or that could have
been the kiss.

Love you,

E

Isle of Skye
18 May 1917

Davey,

I haven't heard from you in a while. I wish I wasn't starting
to feel the first fingers of worry plucking at my heart, the way
they always do when I miss a letter or two from you. You have
to admit, your history in that respect hasn't been exemplary.
When you don't write, it's usually for a reason that makes me
have to sit down to read the letter when it does come—being
wounded and in hospital, being taken prisoner. What is it this
time? What is there left?

I did something different this time. I left Emily with the boys
and I went to church. I didn't go to the stuffy Presbyterian
church of my youth but rather to the tiny Catholic chapel in
Portree. I remembered the warmth and mystery of St. Mary's
and, besides, I thought if I wanted to put in a special request to
God to keep you safe, perhaps I should appeal to the Catholic
God you pray to.

I wasn't the only one in the chapel that day. Other women
were there, in veils and scarves, muttering prayers and lighting
candles. I brought along your little Bible and traced your name
with my fingertip. I lit a candle and, not knowing the proper

prayers, just closed my eyes and thought about you. When I opened them, a woman was sitting by my side, quietly watching me. "Have you said a novena for him?" I admitted I wasn't Catholic, half-expecting her to order me out of the church. Instead, she put her hand on mine and said, "Don't worry. I'll say an extra for you." She gave me her carved wooden rosary and promised to teach me the prayers when she saw me again.

I felt much better after leaving. Even though it is a bit of a journey for me to get to Portree, I now know a place I can go when I want to feel close to you.

Love,
Sue

Isle of Skye
22 May 1917

Davey,

Please quell these fears within me. I have been bicycling to Portree nearly every day to pray for you, and I need some confirmation that my prayers have been answered. These Catholic prayers are newly learned, and I want to be sure I'm doing something right.

Anything, Davey! A postcard. A sentence. A word, even. Please.

Sue

June 1, 1917

Sue,

I've debated for a while about how best to write this to you. You don't know how many versions have ended up in the grate. I suppose the best thing is just to come out and say it.

Iain is alive.

He's not dead, Sue. He's here, in this same camp.

A few weeks ago, we were out having our exercise. A group of British men had recently been transferred to our camp and were clustered on one side of the yard. I tell you, my girl, it brought tears to my eyes to hear English spoken after nothing but French and the occasional indecipherable bit of Russian for six months! I hurried right over to one of the guys, begging to be let in on a conversation, any conversation.

One asked where I was from. I said, "Illinois," and another man called out, "Illinois? You don't say! I have family there. What part?" Europeans never seem to realize the vastness of the United States, so when I said, "Chicago. Urbana, for a while," this guy said to me, "Why, my cousin lives in Chicago! Frank Trimball. Surely you know him? I'll ask him about you. What's your name?"

I told him my name and heard a bellow from somewhere within the throng: "David Graham from Urbana, Illinois?"

I must've responded, Sue, because the next thing I knew, I was on the ground with a stinging cheek and grit in my eyes.

I heard someone say, "What'd you do that for, mate?" and I stood up, still reeling, to see a stranger, his fists clenched, his mouth twisted.

"That was for falling in love with my wife."

Dizzy, I didn't react quickly enough to avoid the second punch.

"And that was for making her fall in love with you."

I spat blood. "Who the hell are you?" I asked, already guessing the answer.

"Elspeth's husband. Or have you gone after so many married women you lost track?"

You really didn't think I could let that comment slide by, now, did you, Sue? Of course I went after him. What followed could only be described as an old-fashioned schoolyard brawl.

It seemed to go on for ages, but it was probably only a matter of minutes before we heard shouts in German and the others finally succeeded in pulling us apart.

We collapsed in the dust, panting, and the crowd dispersed. Truth to tell, we were too tired, too hungry, and too demoralized to do much more.

"Why did you leave her? Why didn't you write?" I had to ask, for your sake. "She thought you were dead."

Iain knuckled his nose. His hand came away bloody. "She had you."

Sue, he knew. The whole time. He found your letters, knew you'd been writing to me in secret for years. He divined all the hints between the lines that we both later found. He guessed how we felt before either of us admitted it. Why do you think he joined up so quickly? Why do you think he was so eager to get to the front? He didn't feel he had anything more to lose.

I don't know yet what this means for us. I'm still wrestling with my own conscience, so I understand if you don't write

back right away. If you want to write to him, he's at the same
address.

David

Isle of Skye
18 June 1917

What a horrible joke that was, Davey! I fainted cold on the
floor when I started to read your letter. Brave Allie had his coat
on, ready to run to town in the rain for the doctor, when I came
to and reassured him that it was nothing but a mean joke.

It was, wasn't it? Iain can't be alive. All those letters I received confirming his death. My separation allowance turned
into a widow's pension. How could the War Office be wrong in
this?

How am I supposed to feel? My husband joins up and heads
out to battle as a grand attempt at suicide. He doesn't write; he
doesn't come to see me. He's been prisoner for over a year now,
without a word to me or to his mother that he was alive. Is he
surprised I fell in love with another man? Wouldn't any woman
do the same?

Oh, Davey! I can't go through this. I can't go through all of
this.

Sue

Kriegsgefangenen-Sendung, Postkarte
June 23, 1917

Sue,

Tomorrow I spread my wings. It may be a while before I
write again, but don't worry about me. You are the blossom that
I fly toward.

I miss your smile.

Davey

June 24, 1917

Sue, my dearest girl,

If you're reading this, it means that Iain has gotten through.
I know it must have been a shock to find him on your doorstep,
resurrected from the grave, so to speak. But I once made you a
promise that I wouldn't stand in the way once he returned home
to you.

I've written a fairy story for you, Sue. I trust that it makes
clear what I cannot. Always know that I love you.

Forever yours,

David

THE FISHERMAN'S WIFE

There was once a fisherman who had a beautiful wife named Lucinda. He'd sail off for weeks, following the fish, and Lucinda waited back on the shore, dangling her bare feet in the waves and making his nets. She wove and knotted the strong silvery threads and, as she wove, she would sing. She sang lonely songs of the sea, spirited sailing shanties, and achingly beautiful melodies that sounded as if they came from the mermaids themselves. But as she gazed out across the water, eyes fixed on the horizon for her husband's boat, each of her songs was tinged with sadness.

Lucinda was so lovely and her song so pure that a water sprite had fallen in love with her. Every day while she sat by the water knotting her nets, the sprite floated nearby, watching her and growing more in love. With each crystal tear that Lucinda shed into the sea, the sprite swam a little closer, wishing there was a way to make her smile. He became determined to win her love and bring her to live in the sea with him.

The sprite swam out to sea, in search of the most precious gifts he could find, things Lucinda had never seen in her humble land, things that would make her realize there was more to the world than her little stretch of shore and the empty horizon. Once she saw how far the sea reached and how much hid beneath the waves, she'd come with him.

He dove to the deepest depths and found the most beautiful conch shell he could, large and creamy white, with a faint glow of pink and pale blue radiating from the inside. He brought it to Lucinda with a shy smile and was pleased to get one in return.

But she refused the gift, saying, "If I want a beautiful shell, I

only need to walk along the beach and choose from the shells scat-
tered there."

"None will be as lovely as this conch shell from so far away."

"They will be lovelier because they are right outside my door."

The next day, the sprite danced through the waves until he found
the most dazzling fish, with trailing fins of bright blue and yellow.
He caught it up in a glass bowl and brought it to Lucinda, who
smiled but answered as before. "If I want to see a dazzling fish, I
only need to look into the shallows of the bay."

"None will be as dazzling as this fish from beyond the waves."

"It will be even more dazzling because it is right outside my
door."

Undeterred, the sprite swam all day and night to a beach in an
exotic land ringed with waving palm trees and the smell of fruit. The
sand along the beach glittered pure white. He scooped up a measure
of the sparkling sand and brought it to Lucinda. But, as before, she
answered, "If I want to see glittering sand, I only have to look down
at this beach."

"It won't be as glittering or as pure white as this sand I found for
you."

"It will be even more glittering in my eyes because it is right out-
side my door." She gave the sprite a kind smile. "The sea is yours.
You go with the current, traveling across the waves to faraway
places. But the sea isn't mine and never can be. My home on the
beach is more precious to me than any of the treasures in the world."

The sprite swam furiously away. He didn't understand how, with
all the magnificent treasures he'd offered her, with the life he could
give her beneath the sea, Lucinda still preferred the company of a
mere fisherman and their simple life on this simple shore. The song

*she sang from the shore, soaring on the wind, was one of yearning
and loss.*

*Rejected, the sprite struck the surface of the water, causing a storm
to rise up in his anger. Rain streamed down, hiding the shoreline behind a curtain of gray. Out at sea, a tiny fishing boat bobbed in the
roiling water. As the water rose, a water horse—bare-chested, sharp-
fanged, seaweed tangled in his mane—strode up the crest of a wave.
White spray behind him, the water horse flew straight toward the boat.*

*The fisherman, pulled beneath the surface, could never come
home. The sprite would never have to fight for Lucinda's love again.
But her song rose above the thunder and crashing waves, and the
sprite knew what he had to do. He dove beneath the surface.*

*He made it to the side of the boat just as the water horse reared
up with saltwater dripping from clawed hooves. The sprite kicked his
legs and shot out of the water like a fish, between the water horse and
the fisherman crouched on the bottom of the boat. The claws of the
water horse sank into the sprite.*

*With all of his power, the sprite blew a wind that pushed the lit-
tle fishing boat back toward shore. He knew that no gift could draw
Lucinda away from her home. But, by sending the fisherman back to
it, he'd found the only gift that mattered.*

Isle of Skye
17 August 1917

Davey,

This man—this *stranger* who appeared on my doorstep—is
not my husband. When he left three years ago, my husband was

strong and arrogant and preoccupied. The smouldering in his eyes that I mistook for fanaticism I now know to be the smouldering of jealousy. But this man, this strange man you sent to me—he's thin, nervous, starving, apologetic, tentative. He's none of the things that Iain was. I don't know who he is.

He said you planned some grand escape. That you stitched up fake uniforms and planned to just walk out of the front gate of the prison camp. That he was the only one who made it.

I want to know, what right do you and Iain have to make my decision for me? What would make you think I would choose to take him back? What would make you think I wouldn't be waiting for *you*?

I don't know what to do with him. He sits in the cottage all day, seemingly ill at ease. He smokes and twitches and weeps when he tries to make love to me. When I pull on my boots to go outside, he grabs on to my apron, as if he expects me to walk out the door and never return.

I've thought about it. But, really, where would I go? I don't know whether you're still a prisoner. I don't know why you sounded so cold in the letter you sent with Iain. I don't know if you are still in love with me. I don't know if you will even open this letter and read it.

Every time I'm in Portree, I stop in the Catholic chapel. I pray you are safe, wherever you may be, and I pray that everything will right itself. Nothing is the way it should be now.

Davey, I need you. You have no idea how much I need you. Nothing is right without you. I need to make my *own* choice.

Sue

Chapter Twenty-six

⌁

Margaret

London
Friday, 20 September 1940

Gran,

I've found her! Oh, my mother, looking so small and pale in that hospital bed. The doctor said that she was in the Langham when it was hit, but she escaped without too many injuries. She has a few broken ribs, a sprained ankle, and a touch of nervous exhaustion. They were afraid of pneumonia, but she seems to have escaped that.

I went by the hotel first, thinking they'd have no idea where she was. But Mother's been there for two months, going out for walks every day, stopping at the desk on her way in to ask if there'd been anything in the post for her. They know her. The clerk gave me the name of the hospital and wished her well.

She was sitting up when I walked in, her hands pressed to her temples, crying. But the moment she saw me, she said, "My Margaret. There you are," and lay right down. The nurses said she hasn't been able to settle since she was brought in, but after she saw me, she slept for almost a whole day.

I'll stay with her and write again to let you know how she's doing, but the doctor doesn't seem concerned that she's in any danger. He's glad that she has family come to care for her. All she needs right now is time and our prayers.

Love,

Margaret

London
Friday, 20 September 1940

Dear Paul,

I've found her at last. And she's as well as can be expected. She was in the Langham when it was hit, though she's not too badly hurt. She wants to go back to Edinburgh something fierce. They need the bed in the ward, what with more injured coming in every day from the air attacks, so they're willing as long as she's not alone.

Right now she's asleep. She lay down straightaway when I arrived and fell asleep with a smile on her lips. The head sister could see I'd come a long way—I was still in my grey traveling suit—and she let me sit by Mother as long as I was quiet and didn't disturb the other patients. She thinks Mother will sleep better with me here.

They said that, when she was taken from the building, she was clutching a suitcase. Only one. She left the other behind but wouldn't let go of the brown suitcase. Even without opening it, I knew why.

Mother snored and murmured in her sleep, and that brown suitcase watched me from under her cot. I knew that I shouldn't. That obediently filial part of me felt guilty even considering opening the suitcase. But the part of me that tossed caution to the wind and wrote to an estranged uncle, that set off for the Isle of Skye with nothing but the name of a house scribbled in the flyleaf of a book, that rushed down to London to dig for my mother through the rubble and bring her home, that part of me kissed Mother's limp hand on the blanket and opened up the suitcase.

They wrote to each other for years, Paul. My mother and Davey. And every letter from him was in there. From the first in 1912—an admiring fan letter from an impetuous college student—to the last in 1917—a scribbled note, grimy from a prison camp, that ended their relationship. Just like that. One moment they were looking to the future, the next he broke it off with a fairy story about a fisherman's wife.

The story was about her. Her husband, Iain, was a fisherman on Skye. He went missing during the war, was declared dead, and reappeared. Turned up on her doorstep with Davey's letter in hand. She didn't even get a choice.

The Next Morning

I wrote that to you and then, as the sunrise came orange through the window, I fell asleep too. When I woke, Mother sat propped up in her bed, watching me covered in her letters.

"You've read my story," she said. I asked if she was angry, but she shook her head. "It wasn't right of me to keep it. It's your story too."

My mind was full of questions, but seeing her there, pale against the pillows, eyes still on the letters, I couldn't. Instead, I asked how she was feeling.

She straightened, but I caught a wince. "So much better. I think I'll be going home soon."

I told her I wasn't sure about that, that the doctor might think it best that she stay and rest awhile longer, but she blinked and sighed. "I just want to go home, Margaret. I've been away for too long." She wiped her eyes with a thumb. "I never should've left. I need to go back to Edinburgh, go on my walks, go sit in the quiet of the cathedral. I don't know how better to build up my strength. Home."

"Elspeth," said a voice from the foot of the bed. "I'll take you home."

If you can believe it, Paul, it was Uncle Finlay. He came.

Love,

Margaret

London
Saturday, 21 September 1940

Dear Gran,

Uncle Finlay came here, to London. He arrived this morning and has spent all day with Mother, catching up on the past two decades without saying much of anything at all. He's taking her home tomorrow, back to Edinburgh.

I don't know how you did it, convincing him to come down to London, to finally talk to Mother, but thank you. For the first time in a while, I see a moment of peace on her face.

Love,

Margaret

London
Sunday, 22 September

Dear Paul,

Last night, before she fell asleep, Mother told me that I had only half the story. I had Davey's letters but not hers.

So, instead of heading to the train station this morning with her and Uncle Finlay, I went to the Langham to see if they'd unearthed her other suitcase. Inside, she told me, were her copybooks, where she jotted drafts of all her letters. Ever the writer.

They had her other suitcase, full of the copybooks. Her half of the story. But, oh, Paul, they also had a letter for her.

To one of the many letters she sent out over the months of waiting in London, someone had sent a reply.

And I don't know what to do. It's her letter, to be sure, but I saw her spread out on that hospital bed, tired and defeated, saw her limping to the train station on her brother's arm, just wanting to put London behind her. What if this reply is nothing? Or, God forbid, bad news?

I'm back to Edinburgh on the next train. I'll have seven and a half hours to decide whether to give her the letter or open it myself.

Love,

Margaret

Detroit, Michigan
September 10, 1940

Dear Mrs. Dunn,

I apologize for not replying sooner, but your letter was forwarded on to me from the secretary of our central branch of the American Field Service Association. They thought I would be in a better position to answer your questions.

I wish I had better news for you, but I do not have any contact information for David Graham. He's never sent updates or news to our bulletin, nor has he attended any of our reunion dinners.

I do have a little bit of information, though, that may help you. Some of the other men kept in touch after the war. And I saw him in Paris. Ol' Dave, he made it through the war. He always was a lucky one.

Dave—we called him "Rabbit"—was in a prison camp for a

few years. He must have been taken prisoner in '16, before the
United States entered the war and the Red Cross took over the
Field Service. He didn't write to any of us, other than his good
friend Harry, while in the camp. But I know he did make it out
after the Armistice. After the war, we all saw him in Paris.

They'd tucked him in a hospital in Paris to get his strength
back before sending him home, but Rabbit snuck out. He caught
up with us at our headquarters at Rue Raynouard. Imagine our
surprise! He was in good shape for having spent time in a prison
camp. He begged a spare suit of clothes and our pocket change
and all the chocolate bars he could carry, then said he wasn't
going home, not yet. He had to go up to Scotland after his girl.

You see, Mrs. Dunn, I recognized your name. No disrespect
intended, but Rabbit could never shut up about you. He was
head over heels. To hear him talk, you were every fairy-tale
princess wrapped up in one. Harry kept mum about the whole
deal, but the rest of us, we knew something had soured during
those years he was at the camp. And then Rabbit turned up at
Rue Raynouard, begging money so that he could go up to Scotland and apologize for something. I guess that was the last time
you saw him too.

But some of the other guys kept in touch after we all got
home to the States. Rabbit went back to teaching. He stayed in
Chicago for a while, then went to Indiana to be nearer to his sister; I'm not sure where he ended up from there. I do know that
he published a book, a fairy-tale book for children. You
should've seen all of us old guys grinning like kids when someone brought it along to an AFSA reunion dinner. Our Rabbit, a
published writer!

I'm sorry that I don't have an address for him, but I thought you'd like to know that he was doing well last I heard of him and that he had a book published. And, although I don't have Rabbit's address, here's Harry Vance's. He's much better than Rabbit at keeping in touch. Harry has been teaching at Oxford. That's not too far from London, is it?

I wish you the best of luck, Mrs. Dunn. And, if you see Rabbit again, please give him my best.

Sincerely,

Billy "Riggles" Ross

Secretary, Midwest Branch,

American Field Service Association

Edinburgh

Tuesday, 24 September 1940

Dear Mr. Vance,

I am writing on behalf of my mother, Mrs. Elspeth Dunn. She has been trying to locate the whereabouts of David Graham, whom she knew years ago. I was given your address by Billy Ross with the American Field Service Association. He thought that you might have current contact information for Mr. Graham.

Please, anything that you can tell me would be welcome. My mother has been looking for Mr. Graham for quite some time. We would both be more grateful than you could know.

Sincerely,

Margaret Dunn

Oxford
27 September

Dear Miss Dunn,

I debated whether or not to send you Dave's address. Old recluse that he is, he values his privacy. But he's spent far too long alone, feeling sorry for himself. He's spent far too long wishing he could change the past.

His address is below. He's been living in London, at a flat around the corner from the Langham Hotel. He always did say that London was full of memories.

Harry Vance

Chapter Twenty-seven

~

Elspeth

Isle of Skye
1 May 1919

Dear David,

    You're probably surprised to be getting this from me, but with my newest book of poetry out, how could I forget one who was once my "fan"?

    Not having heard from you these two years past, I have no idea where in the world you might be. I am hoping that, by sending this parcel to your parents' house, it will get to you somehow.

    How have you been since the war? I wrote to you in the prison camp, soon after Iain returned home, but you never responded. Have you been well?

    It's very odd, but a few months ago I thought I saw you, standing in the road across from my parents' house. I glanced down and then the image was gone. You do know that this island is populated by the spirits and ghosts of memory, don't you?

Iain's recently passed away. Of all the ironies—he makes it through Festubert, through captivity in Germany, through escape and flight, only to die of influenza back at home in his bed. He hadn't been strong since he returned, though, and he fell ill so easily. It was not too surprising when it happened.

Do you know, I think he was waiting to die. He always believed he should have fallen with his friends at Festubert. Things just weren't the same for him once he got home. I don't think he felt as if he fit in. He never seemed to know what to do, especially when it came to me. We tried. We really tried, Davey. Everything was different, but we tried.

I haven't been able to write any poetry in years. "Repose" was one of the last poems I wrote. I couldn't figure out what the problem was, but then I realised.

It was you, Davey. It *is* you. There is no poetry in my life without you. You have been my muse all along. Before I met you, I wrote poetry with my pen, and my readers loved it. It meant something to them. But after meeting you, I wrote poetry with my soul, and *I* loved it. It meant the world to me.

I understand I know nothing of your life now. It's been two years since I've heard anything from you. For all I know, you could be married, have a family. But I'm going to take a page out of your book. I'm going to close my eyes and run right over that trench wall.

Davey, I can't be without you. I can't *be* without you. Do

you remember all of those promises and dreams we made back during the war? Come and make them all again to me.

We'll go wherever you want, live wherever you want. Edinburgh? Skye? Urbana, Illinois? I could go anywhere with you by my side. I'll be your wife, your mistress, your lover. As long as I am yours.

I am closing up my cottage and heading to Edinburgh. Nothing has been right for Màthair since Finlay left. Maybe if I go too, he'll come back. I can do that much at least for her. Will you come to Edinburgh? Will you come to get me?

I'll go to St. Mary's every morning to wait for you. I don't know when you'll get this letter, but I promise I'll wait. I'll wait every morning, as long as it takes. I gave up on you once, that day when Iain, instead of you, walked through the door. I won't give up on you again.

I have never stopped loving you, Davey.

Sue

Chapter Twenty-eight

~

Margaret

Edinburgh
Tuesday, 1 October 1940

Dear Mr. Graham,

I hope you won't think me forward, but I wanted to write to
express my admiration for your book, *Favorite Fairy Stories for
Favorite Children*. Although it has been many years since I've
been young enough for fairy stories, something made me look
beyond the words on the page. Each has a story beneath. Alle-
gory, to be sure, but also magic and poetry. These are not tales
just for children.

I especially was taken with the last in the book, "The Fisherman's Wife." That one felt so real, as though it was written
from the heart. How like life, where we fumble our way through
love only to find that it's simpler than we think.

I find it interesting that you changed the ending of "The

Fisherman's Wife." Originally, you had the story end with
the water sprite sacrificing himself so that the fisherman could
swim safely to shore. A very noble ending. But here, in the published version, you have the water sprite fight for Lucinda's
love. He gives her a chance to choose him of her own free will.
Perhaps not as noble, but real, steeped in regret and hopeful-
ness.

Of course, the tales in this book aren't the only ones you've
written. More than two decades ago, you wrote a love story in
letters, a love story just as magical as the fairy stories—even
more so because it was true. It's a story without an ending,
though. A story that breaks off in one noble moment, leaving
questions for all the moments that came before. Questions that
remain twenty-three years later.

I know you can finish it. You're one of the two best writers I
know.

> With much admiration,
> Margaret Dunn

London, England
October 5, 1940

Dear Miss Dunn,

It seems like a lifetime ago that I first wrote those same three
words. That lifetime has taken me across an ocean, over the
trenches, into hell and back. But writing that "noble ending"
was by far the hardest thing. Little wonder that I changed my
mind.

Only one copy of the original draft ever existed. Please, how is she?

David Graham

Edinburgh
Tuesday, 8 October 1940

Dear Mr. Graham,

She's wondering. She's spent the past twenty-three years wondering why you stopped writing. Why you never replied to the letters she sent after Iain came home. Why you disappeared.

My mother never told me about you or about her life before I was born. But I could see the weight of regret on her shoulders, so many years of wondering and waiting. This war, it's shaken her. It made her remember the other war, she said. Made her remember what she gained and what she lost. War is impulsive, she told me, and you are left with nothing but ghosts.

And maybe it's not my place, to write so to a stranger, but I feel as if I know you—after reading all of her letters, kept walled up since the last war ended. Even though we've never met, I understand you. I'm just as restless, just as fearless, just as searching for my place in the world. I understand questioning but not leaving without a backwards glance. Why did you?

Sincerely,

Margaret Dunn

London, England
October 11, 1940

Dear Margaret,

I didn't stop writing to her. I never could. I regretted that "noble ending" the moment I penned it. I wrote her letter after letter, but with no reply. Why would she want to write back to me when she had her husband back at home? When they had a second chance? Why would she want to write back to me when she had you?

She never wrote another letter, but he did: Iain, he asked me to stop. He asked me to never write again.

After he got back, he said, she was happy. They were starting over and trying to make things work. They'd started a family, something she dearly wanted to do. And it made sense. Why would she want a kid like me? A kid who couldn't settle down? Who didn't want to commit to a family the way she did? No wonder she was glad for Iain to come home.

I did try once to apologize, face-to-face. Even though Iain didn't want me to talk to her again, even if I figured she didn't want to talk to me either, Sue was worth it. When I got out of the camp after the Armistice, I begged, borrowed, and stole to get up to Skye. I had to hear it from her.

Someone directed me to her parents' cottage. When I got there, I heard laughter, and I stopped in the road. I'd never forgotten the sound of Sue's laughter. I looked to the back of the cottage, and I saw her. Sue was with Iain and a little girl. You. Iain had swung you out over a stream, and you were giggling uncontrollably. All three of you laughing. I hesitated. Sue looked up, just for a moment, and I thought she saw me, but then you started to giggle again and I couldn't move a step. I couldn't intrude on that happy family moment. I couldn't intrude on her new life. I left and never tried to contact her again.

All of those letters while I was in the camp, unanswered. And, in all these years, she's never tried to find me. Why stir things up now?

David Graham

Edinburgh
Monday, 14 October 1940

Dear Mr. Graham,

I looked through every letter she saved, and they stopped the day Iain came home. You say you wrote to her. If they'd arrived, why wouldn't she have saved them?

What if she never saw them? Iain might have tossed every one into the fire. You, who won her heart with nothing but your pen: Why would he let them get through?

She said you've always been the only one for her. Her love, her muse, her poetry. When Iain died, she took a risk the way you did. Sent a letter and crossed her fingers. She wrote that she was moving to Edinburgh and that she'd wait for you every day in St. Mary's Cathedral—your old meeting spot—until you arrived. Because you would. You'd get her letter and you'd come for her. She was sure of it.

So sure that she's waiting there now, the way she has every

day since. She's never given up on you. She couldn't go for the noble ending.

Margaret Dunn

London, England
October 17, 1940

Dear Margaret,

Waiting at St. Mary's, all these years?

You know, I'm not surprised. She was always stubborn as a barnacle. Elspeth never gave up on anything—even when she should've given up on me.

I never did get that last letter of hers, the one where she talks of moving to Edinburgh. I've found it now. It was nothing but my own pigheadedness that kept me from reading it before. You see, she sent it tucked in the pages of *Out of Chaos,* her last book. Out of chaos. That seemed to describe Iain to a T. He'd escaped the trenches and a prison camp. He'd left his one rival behind bars. He came home to peace.

From the moment Iain and I met in that prison camp, we were at an impasse. He realized that all was not lost—not with me behind a fence—and I realized that things wouldn't be so easy with Elspeth, not with her husband still alive. I once made her a promise that, if Iain came home, I'd back off.

I was in on an escape plan with a few other guys. We fabricated "Boche uniforms" out of jacket linings, parts of blankets, sheets. Our plan was to put them on and walk straight out of the gate. Audacious, but that was me back then. Iain got wind of the plan and he wanted in. The other guys saved me from having to say a word. They told Iain there wasn't room for him. They said "no" so that I didn't have to.

But it didn't feel right. Here I was, writing to Sue, dreaming about the day I'd see her again, while her husband drew more and more inside himself, knowing he wouldn't. Once again, he'd given up. To sit and watch that and know you are the cause . . . I couldn't do it.

The night before the escape, I wrote "The Fisherman's Wife," with the ending that you read. I folded it in a letter, reminding her of the promise I'd made, to not get in the way if Iain ever returned. I tucked the letter and story in the fake uniform and left it under Iain's pillow.

It wasn't until he got up to Skye and Sue wrote, asking what right we had to make the decision for her, that I began to doubt what I did. I wrote her, oh, so many times. I kept writing until Iain asked me to stop. Until he told me that she didn't care.

Why did I believe him? I don't know. His story that she was happy with him home made sense. He'd come through so much just to be with her. He'd come out of chaos. Hence the title of her book. And I couldn't read a book about Iain, for Iain. He'd taken from me the one thing I needed most of all in the world.

But I was wrong. She did write me again. And not only that letter, tucked in the pages next to "Repose." She wrote me a whole book. Every poem in *Out of Chaos*—from the blushing to the yearning to the missing—was about us. If I'd opened that book all those decades ago, I would've seen that she hadn't given up on me. Her last plea, her last prayer, bound in leather the color of red jasper. She never forgot.

All I had to do was open the book, read everything she wrote for me over the years. But I didn't. Again, I let her down. Again, I showed myself a coward when it mattered most.

    David

Edinburgh
Saturday, 19 October 1940

Dear David,

One letter I found in her copybooks, she never sent. She was writing it the day Iain walked back through her door. One letter that, more than all the rest, reveals. Read it, and then come up to Edinburgh. Read it and come home to us. . . .

    Love,
    Margaret

Isle of Skye
10 August 1917

Dear Davey,

I know I haven't written in a long while, but, please believe me, I've had good reason. What I'm about to admit to you may make you cross, but please don't be angry. I had my reasons.

I told you I lost the baby. But, as my mother says, "The thing about lost items is that someday you may find them again."
I never had a miscarriage, Davey. I had the baby.

Oh, I tried to miscarry. After I got the letter from Harry saying you were dead, I didn't want that reminder, that slap in the face, mocking me with the family I could have had. So I tried to miscarry. I did all of the things they say you're not supposed to do during pregnancy—washing windows, walking over a suicide's grave, eating green plums, standing outside beneath a new moon, drinking whisky while taking a hot bath. Nothing worked.

Then you were alive, and all was perfect. I had my baby, I had my Davey. But I remembered how you felt before, how scary you found the idea of impending fatherhood. I couldn't admit that I found the idea of impending motherhood every bit as scary. And so I put off telling you. And then again. And then again. It got to the point where I couldn't confess my lie without it sounding utterly fictitious. "I hope you enjoyed the parcel of food. Oh, by the way, I gave birth yesterday."

I wish I had told you. I wanted you by my side during the birth. I wanted you to kiss my forehead and tell me that I was doing well, that I was your brave girl. I wanted you to hold your daughter and be the first person she saw when she opened her eyes.

I named her Margaret, which means "pearl." She truly is a treasure.

But things have been hard. I can't lie, Davey. All of the neighbours know. They watched my swelling belly beneath my widow's weeds and they whispered behind their hands. They'd seen the years of letters from America and the three momentous days when Elspeth Dunn stepped on a ferry. They weren't surprised when a bairn came a year after the letter saying Iain had died.

I'm thinking of leaving, tying Margaret to my back and stepping on that ferry one last time. Away from Skye, I can raise her without whispers. Away from Skye, maybe Finlay will return. Màthair misses him so.

You once said that apartment in Edinburgh felt like home. Could we make it so? Come home to Margaret; come home to me. Come home to your family, Davey.

  Waiting,

  Sue

Chapter Twenty-nine

~

Elspeth

Edinburgh
25 October 1940

Dear Màthair,

Margaret has been searching for the first volume of my life; all along, I've been waiting for the second.

On the train back from London, I decided that was enough. No more waiting. No more second volume. What had it brought me? Nine thousand days waiting in the cathedral, a daughter who didn't know the past, and a brother who didn't want to. On the train I had Finlay beside me and Margaret following with the letters. And both were more important than waiting for a ghost.

But then Finlay left me in Edinburgh and I forgot all my promises. Without realizing, my feet traced their usual path to

St. Mary's. I wasn't surprised to look up and see the carved doors. I don't know if my waiting is a drug or a routine, but I couldn't stop with nothing but bold words.

On Wednesday, I was there, in my usual pew, my little brown Bible on my lap, the "David Graham" scrawled in round childish letters inside the cover. As I always did, I traced the backwards "d" at the end of his name, and, as I always did, I promised that this was my last. Nine thousand days is a lot, but ten thousand is excessive. I had to be done. You see, Màthair, that evening I had started to see ghosts.

Only moments earlier, as I crossed York Place in front of the cathedral, I bumped into a man, right there on the street. And, oh, Màthair, my heart leapt.

That same sandy hair, the same hunched shoulders, the same thumbnail creeping up to his mouth. Eyes the brown-green of the hills in wintertime. I would've sworn on my soul it was him.

But a bus rattled past, horn blaring, and he touched his hat before hurrying across the street. I stood frozen for a moment longer, wondering how I could be so mistaken. I was *sure* it was him. But the traffic, hurrying home before the blacked-out streets grew dark, swerved around me, and I knew I had to give up.

In the cathedral, finger tracing the name in the Bible, I swore it was the last time. And, Màthair, I meant it.

I sat until the church grew dark, until someone slipped into the seat next to me: my Margaret, with a new green hat perched on her head. She's moved from home, and I miss her already. Last week, when her Paul had leave, they married. A quick ceremony, an even quicker honeymoon in the Borders, and now she's mistress of her own house. That night, when she slipped next to me in the pew, she wore a secret smile.

"I just came to deliver something." She set an envelope, crisp and square, on top of my Bible. "A special delivery."

Envelopes. Always envelopes in my life. I started shaking before I even saw the name on the outside.

To Sue.

My hands trembled and I dropped it twice before I could get a finger under the flap. I tore the envelope nearly in half.

The letter was short, written on one side of a sheet in scrawled pencil, the handwriting as familiar as my own.

London, England
October 23, 1940

Dear Sue,

Letters are where we started; letters are where we ended. Perhaps, with a letter, we can begin again? I have twenty-three years to tell you about and not enough paper.

I have never stopped loving you.

Davey

The words blurred.

Margaret took my hands. "Mother . . . " She nodded towards the back of the cathedral.

A Highland lass expects to see ghosts. You taught me that.

And yet, when he stepped into the candlelight of the aisle, my breath caught in my teeth. Of all the things I expected, not that, not there, not then.

It *was* him. Those eyes, startled wide. The thumbnail already creeping into his mouth. Looking the way he did the day we met. My Davey. Oh, Màthair, he came. He came.

Eyes brown-green, like the hills in wintertime, fixed on mine. My looking-glass self. Suddenly I didn't feel a day older.

I stood, the little Bible falling from my lap. The letter crinkled in my hand. I stepped towards him, with Margaret, the war, and the whole rest of the world forgotten.

"Hi, Sue." He held out his hand. "Here I am."

I fell into his arms. "There you are, Davey. There you are."

Acknowledgments

Though the first draft of *Letters from Skye* was written in secret, late at night after the rest of the family had fallen asleep, it would not be where it is today without the support and encouragement of many.

My sincere thanks to all of the readers who helped my novel soar, especially Bryn Greenwood and Christine Roberts. To Elaine Golden, for the last, perfect line. To Sue Laybourn and Louise Brennan, for giving my characters the right words. To Richard Bourgeois, for reads, cheers, and sea monsters. To Kate Langton, for unflinching faith. I did it. To the Nanobeans, for their irreverence, encouragement, and cheese scones. Since leaving Edinburgh, I've tried to recreate that circle of writerly energy, of support and nonsense and fellowship. I wish I could.

To Danielle Lewerenz, for being my sounding board, my cheerleader, my friend. You helped build Davey into a hero to fall in love with. To Rebecca Burrell, for being there. I'm still not sure how I wrote books before you.

To my agent, Courtney Miller-Callihan, for signing me with such confidence and sending my manuscript out into the world with such conviction. To my editor, Jennifer E. Smith, for seeing in my words the same story I've always seen and for helping me to make it the novel it needed to be. Many thanks to the whole team at Random House/Ballantine, especially the tireless subsidiary rights department.

To my parents and my sister, Becky, for never doubting me. I hope that I've made you proud. To Ellen and Owen, for their patience and their forgiveness when I forget to do the laundry. I love you. To Jim, for Scotland and everything else.

It still amazes me that Elspeth and Davey are just as real to other people as they are to me. Thank you to everyone who helped to bring them to life.

About the Author

JESSICA BROCKMOLE spent several years living in Scotland, where she knew too well the challenges in maintaining relationships from a distance. She plotted her first novel on a long drive from the Isle of Skye to Edinburgh. She now lives in Indiana with her husband and two children.

About the Type

This book is set in Fournier, a typeface named for Pierre Simon Fournier, the youngest son of a French printing family. He started out engraving woodblocks and large capitals, then moved on to fonts of type. In 1736 he began his own foundry and made several important contributions in the field of type design; he is said to have cut 147 alphabets of his own creation. Fournier is probably best remembered as the designer of St. Augustine Ordinaire, a face that served as the model for Monotype's Fournier, which was released in 1925.